# BIGGLES
## *in* FRANCE

# CAPTAIN W.E. JOHNS

**RED FOX**

Red Fox would like to express their grateful thanks
for help given in the preparation of these editions to Jennifer Schofield,
author of *By Jove, Biggles*, Linda Shaughnessy of A. P. Watt Ltd
and especially to the late John Trendler.

BIGGLES IN FRANCE
A RED FOX BOOK 978 0 09 928311 9

First published in Great Britain by Boys' Friend Library, 1935

This Red Fox edition published 2004

15

Red Fox Books are published by Random House Children's Publishers UK
61–63 Uxbridge Road, London W5 5SA,
a division of The Random House Group Ltd

Addresses for companies within The Random House Group Limited
can be found at:
www.randomhouse.co.uk/offices.htm

THE RANDOM HOUSE GROUP Limited Reg. No. 954009

A CIP catalogue record for this book is available from the British Library.

The Random House Group Limited supports The Forest Stewardship
Council (FSC®), the leading international forest certification organisation.
Our books carrying the FSC label are printed on FSC® certified paper.
FSC is the only forest certification scheme endorsed by the leading
environmental organisations, including Greenpeace. Our
paper procurement policy can be found at
www.randomhouse.co.uk/environment

Printed and bound in Great Britain by Clays Ltd, St Ives PLC

# Contents

# Foreword

**Biggles in France** was originally published by *The
Boys' Friend Library* as a cheap paperback in 1935
and has been unavailable ever since. It is
appropriate that this rare collection of short stories
should be reprinted for the first time in their
original form in 1993, the centenary year of W. E.
Johns' birth.

Although Biggles is a fictional character, many of
these early wartime aviation stories were based on the
real life experiences of W. E. Johns and his colleagues
in the Royal Flying Corps (the Royal Air Force from
1 April 1918). Johns' early military career also gave
him an appreciation of the struggles endured by the
ordinary soldier. He entered World War One as a
private in the King's own Royal Regiment, the Norfolk
Yeomanry, and fought in the trenches at Gallipoli,
Turkey. Later he transferred to the machine gun corps
and contracted malaria while based in Macedonia,
northern Greece. While recovering, he heard that the
Royal Flying Corps urgently needed volunteers and
decided to apply, being accepted for basic training as
a pilot in 1917.

After completing a short spell as a flying instructor,
he joined WO55 squadron at Azelot, near Nancy in
France, where he flew the two seater De Havilland 4 on
day bombing raids and photographic reconnaissance
duties over Germany. On 16 September 1918, while on
a bombing mission, his plane was shot down and he

was taken prisoner, his observer/gunner being killed. He made two unsuccessful attempts to escape and was sent to a punishment camp. Days later the war ended and by Christmas 1918, he was back in England.

These personal experiences gave Johns a strong basis for **Biggles in France** and the stories therefore have a particularly authentic atmosphere. He later updated some of these for World War Two and published them in 1941 as **Spitfire Parade**\*. He realised that Biggles had strong potential as a role model for a new generation of post-war readers and dedicated the book to airmen 'in the hope that his [Biggles'] ideals may be an inspiration to them.'

**John Trendler,** *editor* **Biggles and Co** *magazine*

\* Published by Red Fox as a graphic novel

# Chapter 1
# Down to Earth

Second-Lieut. Bigglesworth of No. 266 Squadron, R.F.C.,* stationed at Maranique, France, settled himself in a deckchair, cocked his feet up on the balustrade that ran round the veranda in front of the officer's mess,** yawned lazily in the summer sunshine, and then looked up at the group of pilots who had collected there whilst awaiting the summons of the luncheon gong.

'What do you think about it, Biggles?' asked Mahoney, his flight-commander, fishing a pip from his glass of lemon crush.

'About what?'

'I say that the fellow who goes about this war casually volunteering for this and that has about as much chance of seeing the dawn of peace as a snowball has of surviving midsummer day in the Sahara. Sooner or later he gets it—he's bound to. I could give you scores of instances. Take Leslie Binton, for example—'

'I never heard anyone talk as much drivel as you do,' interrupted Biggles wearily. 'You sit here day after day laying down the law about how to avoid getting pushed out of this world, but do you practise what you preach? Not on your life! If the Old Man*** came

* Royal Flying Corps 1914–1918. An army corps responsible for military aeronautics, renamed the Royal Air Force (RAF) when amalgamated with the Royal Naval Air Service on 1 April 1918.
** The place where officers eat their meals and relax together.
*** Slang: person in authority, the Commanding Officer.

along here now and said he wanted some poor prune to fly upside down at fifty feet over the Boche* Lines**, you'd be the first to reach for your flying togs.

'I'm not saying you're wrong about this volunteer stuff. Personally, I think you're right, because it stands to reason that the pitcher that goes oftenest to the well gets a better chance of being busted than the one that sits on the shelf.'

'Not necessarily,' argued Wells, a Canadian pilot with a good deal of experience who had recently joined the squadron. 'It's just as likely to get knocked off the shelf on to the floor. It's no more true than the proverb about an empty pitcher making the most noise.'

'Are you telling me I'm an empty pitcher?' inquired Biggles coldly.

'Wait a minute—let me finish. What I was going to say was, you're as bad as Mahoney. You say the volunteer act doesn't pay—'

'It doesn't!'

'Then why do you take a pace forward every time a sticky job comes along?'

'To save poor hoots like you from getting their pants scorched.'

'Rot! Well, you go ahead, but anyone in their right mind can get all the trouble they want out here in France without looking for it. All the same, I aim to outlive you guys by at least three weeks.'

There was a sudden stir, and a respectful silence fell as Major Mullen, their C.O.*** and Colonel Raymond,

* A derogatory slang term for the Germans.
** Front line trenches, the place where the opposing armies faced one another.
*** Commanding Officer.

10

of Wing Headquarters* walked up the short flight of stairs from the Squadron Office.

Biggles took one glance at the major's face, caught Mahoney's eye and winked. The C.O. was too young to dissemble, and he showed his anxiety plainly on his face when the squadron was selected for a particularly dangerous task.

He looked around the assembled officers. 'All right, gentlemen, sit down,' he said quietly. 'Is everybody here, Mahoney?' he went on, addressing the senior flight-commander.

'Yes, I think so, sir.'

'Good. I won't waste time beating about the bush, then. I want an officer to—'

Biggles and Mahoney sprang up together. Wells took a pace forward, and several other officers edged nearer the C.O. And Major Mullen smiled.

'No, I shan't want you, Bigglesworth—or you, Mahoney. Wells, you've had a good deal of experience at reconnaissance, haven't you?'

'Yes, sir,' replied Wells eagerly, turning to frown at Biggles, who had tittered audibly.

'Good. Have a word with Colonel Raymond, will you? He will explain what he wants.'

'But sir—' began Biggles. But the C.O. silenced him with a frown.

'I'm not in the least anxious to lose my best pilots,' he said softly, as Wells and the colonel disappeared into the ante-room, and the other officers filed into the dining-room as the gong sounded.

'Gosh! This must be something extra sticky,' growled Biggles to Mahoney, as they followed. 'It would have

---

* The administrative headquarters. Each Wing commanded several squadrons. It was headed by a Lieutenant Colonel.

been a lot more sensible to hand the job to someone—'

'I never heard anyone talk as much drivel as you
do,' mimicked Mahoney, and side-stepped quickly to
avoid the jab that Biggles aimed at him.

'You go and get on with your O.P.*' Biggles told
him sourly.

'Aren't you flying this afternoon?'

'No, my kite's** flying a bit left-wing low, but I may
test her if she is finished in time.'

After lunch, Biggles made his way slowly to the
sheds, where he found the riggers*** putting the last
touches to his machine.

'All right, Flight?' he asked Smyth, his flight-
sergeant.

'She's O.K. now, sir, I think,' replied the N.C.O.†
briskly.

'Fine! Start her up; I'll test her.'

Ten minutes later, at two thousand feet above the
aerodrome, he concluded his test with a couple of flick
loops, and, satisfied that the machine was now rigged
as he liked it, he eyed the eastern sky meditatively.

'There's nothing to do on the floor, so I might as
well take a prowl round,' he decided—and turned his
nose in the direction of the Lines.

Mahoney, sitting at the head of his flight in front of
the hangars, with his engine ticking over in readiness
for the afternoon patrol, watched him go with a curious
expression that was half frown and half smile.

---

* Offensive patrol: actively looking for enemy aircraft to attack.
** Slang: aeroplane.
*** People responsible for the assembly and adjustment of the air frame
and controls.
† Non-commissioned officer e.g. a Corporal or a Sergeant.

'There he goes,' he mused. 'He can't keep out of it. One day, I suppose—'

Not waiting to complete his remark, he shoved the throttle open and sped across the short turf.

For an hour or more Biggles soared in the blue sky, searching for hostile aircraft, or anything to distract him from the irritating attentions of archie (anti-aircraft gunfire), but in vain. The sky seemed absolutely deserted, and he was about to turn back towards the Lines when a movement far below and many miles in enemy country caught his eye.

It was only a tiny flash, and would have passed unnoticed by anyone except an experienced pilot. But he knew that it was the reflection of the sun's rays catching the planes of a banking machine. Instinctively he turned towards it, peering down through the swirling arc of his propeller, and pushing up his goggles to see more clearly.

Presently he made out a whirling group of highly coloured machines, and his lips set in a straight line as he ascertained the reason for their aerobatics. A solitary British machine, a Camel,* with the same markings as his own, was fighting a lonely battle against a staffel** of Albatros*** scouts that swarmed around it like flies round a honey-pot. The pilot was putting up a brilliant fight, twisting and half-rolling as he fought his way inch by inch towards the Lines, but he was losing height rapidly.

Biggles half-closed his eyes, and his top lip curled back from his teeth as he stood his machine on its nose

---

* A single seat biplane fighter with twin machine guns synchronised to fire through the propeller.
** The German equivalent of a Squadron.
*** German single seater fighter with two fixed machine guns.

and plunged down like a bolt from the blue, wires and struts screaming a shrill crescendo wail.

His speed outdistanced his altimeter,* and it was still on the four thousand feet mark when he was down to two thousand, with the tragedy written plain to see. It was Wells, being forced down by ten or a dozen Huns.

A pilot of less courage might well have considered landing in the face of such frightful odds, and thus escape the fate that must, if he persisted, sooner or later overtake him; but apparently no such thought entered Wells' head.

Biggles was still a thousand feet away when the end came. A stream of flame leapt from the side of the Camel, and a cloud of black smoke swirled aft. The pilot, instead of side-slipping into the ground, soared upwards like a rocketing pheasant, in a last wild effort to take his destroyer with him, but the wily Hun pilot saw him coming and swerved in the nick of time.

A sheet of flame leapt back over the cockpit of the stricken Camel as it stalled at the top of its zoom. The pilot, with his arm over his face, climbed out on to the fuselage, stood poised for an instant, then jumped clear into space.**

The Hun pilot, fascinated by the slowly somersaulting leather-jacketed figure, raised his hand in salute, and at that moment Biggles' tracer*** bullets bored a group of neat round holes between the shoulders of the Hun's grey jacket. The Hun, without knowing what had hit him, lurched forward across his control-stick,

---

* An instrument for gauging height above ground.
** Only a very few pilots were given parachutes in the First World War, so to jump from a plane meant a leap to certain death.
*** Phosphorous-loaded bullets whose course through the air could be seen by day or night.

and the Albatross buried itself deep in the ground not a hundred feet from the smoking remains of its victim.

Biggles, pale as death, and fighting mad, swung round just as the leader of the Hun staffel took him in his sights, far outside effective range, and fired a short burst. It was a thousand-to-one chance, but it came off. A single bullet struck Biggles' machine, but it struck one of the few vulnerable spots—the propeller.

There was a vibrating, bellowing roar as the engine, now unbalanced and freed from the brake on its progress, raced and nearly tore itself from the engine bearers.

Biggles, not knowing for a moment what had happened, was nearly flung out by the vibration, but as he throttled back and saw the jagged ends of the wooden blades, he snarled savagely and looked below. There was no help for it; an aeroplane cannot remain in the air without a propeller, so down he had to go.

Immediately he looked below he knew that a crash was inevitable, for his height was less than five hundred feet, and the combat had taken him over a far-reaching forest. He switched off automatically, to prevent the risk of fire, and flattened out a few feet above the treetops for a 'pancake*' landing.

At the last instant, as the machine wobbled unsteadily before dropping bodily into the trees, he raised his knees to his chin and buried his face in his arms.

There was a splintering, tearing crash of woodwork and fabric, a jar that shook every tooth in his head, and then a silence broken only by the receding drone of Mercedes engines.

Slowly he unfolded himself and looked around. The machine, as he had guessed, was caught up in the

* Instead of an aircraft gliding down to land, it flops down from a height of a few feet, after losing flying speed.

15

topmost branches of a large tree, and it swayed unsteadily as he moved.

Remembering that more than one pilot who had crashed in similar circumstances had been killed by falling from the tree, and breaking his neck, Biggles unfastened his safety belt warily and crept to the nearest fork, from where he made his way inch by inch to the trunk. After that it was fairly plain sailing, although he had to jump the last ten or twelve feet to the ground.

In the silent aisles of the forest he paused to listen, for he knew that the Boche pilots would quickly direct a ground force to the spot; but he could hear nothing. A steady rain of petrol was dripping from the tree, and he set about his last duty. He divested himself of his flying coat, which would now only be an encumbrance, and after removing the maps from the pocket, he thrust it far under a bush. Then he threw the maps under the dripping petrol and flung a lighted match after them.

There was a loud whoosh as the petrol-laden air took fire. A tongue of flame shot upward to the suspended Camel, which instantly became a blazing inferno. He sighed regretfully, and then set off at a steady jog-trot through the trees in the direction of the Lines.

A few minutes later the sound of voices ahead brought him up with a jerk, and he just had time to fling himself under a convenient clump of holly bushes when a line of grey-clad troops in coal-scuttle helmets, with an officer at their head, passed him at the double, going in the direction of the source of the smoke that drifted overhead.

Satisfied they were out of earshot, he proceeded on his way, but with more caution. Again he stopped as a clearing came in view, and a low buzz of conversation reached him. He began to make a detour round the

16

spot, but his curiosity got the better of him, and, risking a peep through the undergrowth at the edge of the clearing, he saw a curious sight.

An area of about two acres had been cleared, and in the middle of it four enormous concrete beds had been laid down in a rough line. Three appeared to be actually complete, and a gang of men were engaged in smoothing the surface of the fourth.

He did not stop to wonder at their purpose, but they reminded him vaguely of some big gun emplacements that he had once seen far over the British side of the Lines. Dodging from tree to tree, sometimes dropping to all fours to cross an open place, he pressed forward, anxious to get as near the Lines as possible before nightfall.

Just what he hoped to do when he reached them he did not know, but it was not within his nature to submit calmly to capture while a chance of escape remained. He would consider the question of working his way through the Lines when he reached them.

The sun was already low, when the German balloon line* came into view; far beyond it he could see the British balloons hanging motionless in the glowing western sky. Presently, he knew, they would be hauled down for the night; in fact, the nearest German balloon was already being dragged down by its powerful winch.

He wondered why it was being taken in so early, until the low, unmistakable hum of a Bentley engine reached his ears. Then he saw it, a solitary Camel, streaking in his direction. It was flying low, the British pilot altering his course from time to time, almost as if

* Both sides in the First World War used kite or observation balloons with observers in baskets suspended below the balloon, for spotting gun positions and troop movements. Unlike aircraft, balloons carried parachutes for the crew to use in an emergency.

17

he was picking his way through the dark smudges of smoke that blossomed out around him as the German archie gunners did their best to end the career of the impudent Englishman.

Biggles, watching it as it passed overhead, recognised Mahoney's streamers,* and suddenly guessed the reason for its mission. It was looking for him—or for the crash that would tell his own story—and he smiled grimly as the Camel circled once over the scene that appeared to tell the story of the tragedy only too plainly. Then it turned back towards the Lines and was soon lost in the distance.

'They'll be drinking a final cup to the memory of poor old Wells and myself presently!' he mused, as he hesitated on the edge of a narrow lane that crossed his path. He traversed it swiftly after a quick glance to left and right, and, taking cover by the side of a thick hedge, held on his way.

---

* Streamers were used to make it easy to identify the Squadron Leader or Flight Leader in the air.

# Chapter 2
# A Desperate Chance!

He came upon the Boche balloon party quite suddenly, and crept into a coppice that bordered the lair of the silken monster in order to get a closer view of it. Balloons were common enough in the air, but few pilots were given an opportunity of examining one on the ground.

It was still poised a few feet above the field, with the basket actually touching the turf, and was being held down by the men of the balloon section, who were rather anxiously watching two observers, easily recognised by their heavy flying kit, now talking to the officer in charge a short distance away.

It was easy to deduce what had happened. The balloon had been hauled down when Mahoney's Camel came into sight, and a consultation was now being held as to whether or not it was worthwhile sending it up again. The observers were evidently in favour of remaining on the ground, for they pointed repeatedly to the direction in which the Camel had disappeared, and then towards the kite-balloon.

The balloon had been released from its cable and was straining in the freshening breeze, which, by an unusual chance, was blowing towards the British Lines.

As Biggles realised this, the germ of an idea crept into his mind, but it was so fantastic that he endeavoured to dismiss it. Yet in spite of his efforts the thought persisted. If the balloon was free—as it would be if the crew released their hold on it—it would inevitably be

19

blown over the British Lines, and, naturally, anyone in the basket would go with it.

He did not stop to ponder what would happen when it got there; sufficient for him in his present predicament to know that if in some way he could get into the basket and compel the crew to release their hold on the balloon, he would soon be over friendly country, instead of remaining in Germany with the prospect of staying there for the duration of the War.

Reluctantly he was compelled to dismiss the idea, for to attack the whole balloon section single-handed and unarmed was a proposition that could not be considered seriously. So from his place of concealment he watched the scene for a few minutes despondently, and he was about to turn away to resume his march when a new factor introduced itself and made him catch his breath in excitement.

The first indication of it was the distant but rapidly increasing roar of an aero engine. The balloon crew heard it, too, and evidently guessed, as well as Biggles, just what it portended, for there was a general stir as the men craned their necks to see the approaching machine and tried to drag their charge towards the coppice.

The stir became more pronounced as Mahoney's Camel leapt into view over the trees and swooped down upon the balloon in its lair.

'He's peeved because he thinks I've gone West,* so he's ready to shoot up anyone and anything,' was the thought that flashed into Biggles' brain.

The chatter of the twin Vickers** guns broke into his thoughts, and he watched the scene spellbound, for

* Slang: been killed
** Machine guns firing a continuous stream of bullets at one squeeze of the trigger

20

the stir had become blind panic. Two or three of the crew had fallen under the hail of lead, while several more were in open flight, leaving the balloon in the grip of the few more courageous ones, who shouted for help as they struggled to keep the now swaying gasbag on the ground.

Biggles could see what was about to happen, and was on his feet actually before the plan had been born in his brain, sprinting like a deer across the open towards his only hope of salvation. Out of the corner of his eye he saw Mahoney's Camel twisting and turning as it ran for the Line through a blaze of archie.

He heard a shout behind him, but he did not stop. As a drowning man plunges at a straw in the last frenzy of despair, so he hurled himself at the basket of the balloon. As in a dream, he heard more shouts and running footsteps.

Luckily, the nearest man had his back towards him, and Biggles flung him aside with a mighty thrust. He grabbed the rim of the basket, and, lifting his feet, kicked the second man aside.

Just what happened after that he could never afterwards describe; it was all very confused. He saw the two remaining members of the crew start back, the balloon forgotten in their astonishment and fright, and the next moment he was jerked upwards with such force that he lost his grip with his right hand, and felt sure his left arm would be torn from its socket.

But with the fear of death in his heart he clung on, with the desperation of despair.

Somehow his right hand joined the left on the rim of the basket, and his feet beat a wild tattoo on the wickerwork sides as they sought to find a foothold to take his weight, in order to relieve the tension on his arms and enable him to climb up to comparative safety.

His muscles grew numb with the strain, and just as he felt his strength leaving him, his right knee struck something soft. In an instant his leg had curled round the object, and he made a last supreme effort. Inch by inch he lifted his body, which seemed to weigh a ton, until his chin was level with the rim of the basket; his foot swung up over the edge.

For two seconds he lay balanced, then fell inwards, gasping for breath and clutching at his hammering heart.

For perhaps a minute he could only lie and pant, while perspiration oozed from his face, for the strain had been terrific, and he trembled violently when he tried to rise. Then sheer will-power conquered, and, hauling himself up to the edge of the basket, he looked over the side, only to receive another shock that left him spellbound.

Just what he had expected to see he had not stopped to consider, but he certainly imagined that he would still be within reasonable distance of the ground. That the balloon, freed from its anchor, could shoot up to seven or eight thousand feet in two or three minutes was outside his knowledge of aeronautics. Yet such was the case.

So far below that he could no longer see the spot where he had left the ground, lay the earth, a vast indigo basin that merged into blue and purple shadows at the distant horizon.

'Golly!' he gasped and the sound of his voice in the eerie silence made him jump.

The deep rumble of the guns along the Line, like a peal of distant thunder, was the only sound that reached his ears. He was oppressed by a curious sense of loneliness, for there was nothing he could do except watch his slow progress towards the shell-torn strip of No Man's Land* between the opposing front-line trenches now visible like a long, ugly scar across the western landscape, so he fell to examining his unusual aircraft.

Above loomed the gigantic body of the gasbag: around him hung a maze of ropes and lines. A small drawing-board, with a map pinned on it, was fastened at an inclined angle to one side of the basket, and near it, hanging half over the rim, just as it had been casually thrown by its last wearer, was the complicated webbing harness of a parachute.

He followed the life line and saw that it was connected to a bulging case outside the basket, the same protuberance which had assisted him to climb up when he had been dangling in space.

The parachute interested him, for it represented a means of getting back to earth if all else failed. But he regarded the apparatus with grim suspicion. He had, of course, seen the device employed many times, both on the British and German sides of the Lines, but it had been from a distance, and as a mildly interested spectator. It had never occurred to him that he might one day be called upon to use one.

He fitted the harness over his shoulders, and with some difficulty adjusted the thigh straps. Then he looked over the side again, and for the first time in his life really appreciated the effort of will required to jump into space from such a ghastly height.

A terrific explosion somewhere near at hand brought his heart into his mouth, and he stared upwards under the impression that the balloon had burst.

To his infinite relief he saw that it was still intact, but a smudge of black smoke was drifting slowly past

* The area of land between the opposing armies.

it. He recognised his old enemy, archie, and wondered why the burst made so much noise—until he remembered that he was accustomed to hearing it above the roar of an aero engine; in the deathly silence the sound was infinitely more disturbing.

Another shell, quickly followed by another, soared upwards, and burst with explosions that made the basket quiver. The smoke being black indicated that the shells were being fired by German gunners, so he assumed that they had been made aware of what had occurred and were endeavouring to prevent him from reaching the British Lines.

At that moment a white archie burst flamed amongst the black ones, and he eyed it mournfully, realising that the British gunners had spotted the balloon for a German, and were making good practice on it! To be archied by the gunners of both sides was something that he had never supposed possible!

Slowly, but with horrible certainty, the shells crept nearer as the gunners corrected their aim, and more than once the shrill whe-e-e-e of flying shrapnel made him duck.

'This is no blinking joke,' he muttered savagely. 'I shall soon have to be doing something. But what?'

He had a confused recollection that a balloon had some sort of device which allowed the gas to escape, with the result that it sank slowly earthward. But desperate though the circumstances were, he dared not pull any of the trailing cords, for he knew that there was yet another which ripped a panel out of the top, or side, of the fabric and allowed the whole structure to fall like a stone.

He eyed the dark bulk above him sombrely. Somehow or other he must allow the gas to escape in order to lose altitude, and for a wild moment he thought of

24

trying to climb up the guy-ropes to the fabric and then cutting a hole in it with his penknife; but he shrank from the ordeal.

An extra close burst of archie made him stagger, and in something like panic, he grabbed one of the ropes and pulled it gingerly. Nothing happened. He pulled harder, but still nothing happened.

'Why the dickens don't they fix control-sticks to these kites?' he snarled, and was about to give the rope a harder pull when the roar of an aero-engine, accompanied by the staccato chatter of a machine-gun, struck his ears.

'It looks as if it's me against the rest of the world!' he thought bitterly, as a Camel swept into view.

It banked steeply, a perfect evolution that in other circumstances would have been a joy to behold, and then tore back at him, guns spurting orange flame that glowed luridly in the half-light. It disappeared from view behind the bulk of the gasbag, and with a sinking feeling in his heart he knew that the end of his journey was at hand.

The chatter of the gun made him wince, and, leaning out of the basket, he saw a tiny tongue of flame lick up the side of the bellying fabric.

Now, there are moments in dire peril when fear ceases to exist and one acts with the deadly deliberation that is the product of final despair. For Biggles this was one of them. All was lost so nothing mattered.

'Well, here goes; I'm not going to be fried alive!' he said recklessly, and climbing up on to the edge of the basket, he dived outwards.

As he somersaulted slowly through space, the scene around him seemed to take on the curious aspect of a slow motion film. He saw the balloon, far above, enveloped in a sheet of flame; the Camel was still banking, but so slowly, it seemed, that the thought flashed through his mind that it would stall and fall into the flames.

Then the blazing mass above was blotted out by a curious grey cloud that seemed to mushroom out above him, and he was conscious of a sudden terrific jerk; the sensation of falling ceased, and he felt that he was floating in space on an invisible cushion of incredible softness.

'The parachute!' he gasped, suddenly understanding. 'It's opened!'

Then the Camel swept into sight again from beyond the parachute and dived towards him, the pilot waving a cheerful greeting.

Biggles stared at the markings on the fuselage with comical amazement; there was no mistaking them. It was Mahoney's machine. He smiled as the humour of the situation struck him, and placing his thumb to his nose, he extended his fingers in the time-honoured manner.

Mahoney, who at that moment was turning away, changed his mind and flew closer, as if to confirm the incredible spectacle. But the swiftly falling figure raced him to the earth before he could come up with it again.

Biggles saw with a shock that he was now very close to the ground, and even while he was thinking of the best way to fall he struck it. The wind was knocked out of him, but he was past caring about such trifles. Picking himself up quickly, he saw with relief that the fabric had become entangled in some bushes, which arrested its progress and thus prevented him from being dragged.

It was nearly dark, and strangely quiet, so he assumed that he must have fallen some distance behind the Lines, a state of affairs he was quickly able to confirm from a pedestrian whom he accosted on a road which he came upon after crossing two or three fields.

An hour later, the car he had hired at the nearest village pulled up at Maranique, and, after paying the driver, Biggles walked briskly towards the mess. Noticing that a light was still shining in the Squadron Office, he glanced through the window as he passed, and saw Colonel Raymond in earnest consultation with the C.O. He knocked on the door, and smiled wanly when he saw the amazed expressions on the faces of the two senior officers.

'Good gracious, Bigglesworth!' stammered Major Mullen. 'We thought—Mahoney said—'

'Yes, I know, sir,' broke in Biggles. 'I went down over the other side, but I've managed to get back. I'm sorry to say that poor Wells has gone West, though.'

'What happened?' asked the C.O.

Briefly, Biggles gave him an account of his adventures. When he mentioned, quite casually, the concrete emplacements he had seen in the forest, Colonel Raymond sprang to his feet with a sharp cry.

'You saw them?' he ejaculated.

'Why, yes, sir,' replied Biggles. 'Is there anything remarkable about them?'

'Remarkable! It's the most amazing coincidence I ever heard of in my life!' And then, noting the puzzled look on the faces of the others: 'You see,' he explained, 'we heard that the Boche were bringing up some new long-range guns, and to try to locate them was the mission poor Wells undertook this afternoon! And it's you that's found them—by sheer accident!

'If you will mark them down on the map I'll get back to headquarters right away!'

# Chapter 3

# One Bomb and Two Pockets

At the period when Biggles was just becoming known to other squadrons in France as a splendid fighting pilot, he was often heard to remark that his narrowest escape from being fried alive or from being transformed into 'roast beef'—to use the gruesome but picturesque expression then in vogue—occurred not at the time of his adventure in the German balloon over the enemy's lines, or at any other time in the air, as one might reasonably suppose, but on the ground.

Quite apart from the dangerous aspect of the matter, it put a blot on his otherwise clean record that took some time to erase, for the authorities do not look kindly on those who destroy Government property, or, as in Biggles' case, the person through whose instrumentality such destruction occurs. Nevertheless, to his intimate circle of acquaintances, the affair was not without its humour.

Admittedly, episodes of a similar nature had occurred at other squadrons, these being usually brought about by sheer high spirits or a sense of irresponsibility occasioned by nervous strain. Neither of these excuses helped Biggles, nor did they really apply to his case.

It was unfortunate that the authorities had just decided that such 'pranks' must cease, and Biggles, whose affair immediately followed this decision, was pounced upon as a suitable victim to be made an example of.

In spite of his protests that the whole matter was an accident beyond his control, he was hauled up before a court of 'frosty-faced brass-hats*,' and had a flea put in his ear, as the saying goes. In military parlance, he was reprimanded. There was a good deal of indignation over this in the squadron at the time. But once settled, the affair was never referred to again in Biggles' presence, which may account for the fact that so little is known about it.

It came about this way, and in order to grasp the essential details we must start at the very beginning.

One day about the middle of June, during a brisk period of trench strafing**, Biggles spotted a Boche two-seater making for home. It had evidently been over the British Lines, and was a good deal higher than he was, but there was a fair amount of cloud about, and he thought there was a chance of stalking the enemy before he reached his aerodrome.

He at once gave chase, but, to his chagrin, the Boche—which turned out to be a Roland two-seater fighter***—although he had not seen his pursuer, actually glided down and landed at an aerodrome well behind the Lines, just as Biggles reached the spot.

In his mortification, Biggles looked about him for a means of making his displeasure known, and, remembering that he still had a twenty-pound bomb on his rack, he sailed down and let it go at the unconscious cause of his wrath. He saw at once that the bomb would miss its mark, which annoyed him still more, but, knowing quite well that his single-handed attack

* Slang: senior officers referring to the gold braid on their caps.
** Using his guns to attack the trenches from the air.
*** German two-seater fighter, with the observer/gunner armed with a machine gun.

would most certainly stir up a hornets' nest, he turned and made full-out for home.

He had not been back at Maranique for more than an hour when a dark-green Boche, who had evidently slipped over high up with his engine cut off, hurtled down out of the clouds above the aerodrome. Everyone sprinted for cover, but the anticipated attack did not materialise. Instead, the Boche, which Biggles now saw was the same Roland two-seater that he had recently pursued, dropped a small packet with a streamer attached.

This, when picked up, was found to contain a letter, the gist of which was to the effect that Biggles' bomb had hit the carefully constructed private 'bomb-proof' wine-store of a certain Lieutenant von Balchow, with disastrous results to its highly prized contents.

This, it was stated, was a knavish trick, and the officer responsible for dropping the bomb was invited to pay for the wine or meet the owner in single combat at an appointed spot at a certain time. Von Balchow was evidently a scion of an ancient family who believed in the duel as the 'grand manner' of settling personal disputes!

Biggles had no intention of paying for the wine—he could not have done so had he wished. But he was by no means adverse to having a 'stab' at the noble Von Blachow at any old time and place he liked to name.

In this admirable project, however, he was shouted down by such old-timers as Mahoney and Maclaren, who saw in the carefully prepared missive a sinister plot inviting a young British officer to come and be killed.

'This sort of thing has happened before,' Mahoney told him bitterly. 'But the fellow who has gone out to meet the other chap has seldom come back. If you want to know the reason, I'll tell you. The thing is simply a trap, and I very much doubt if you hit the wine-store.

'Even in the event of your meeting the other fellow—which is doubtful—the rest of the bunch will be "upstairs" waiting to carve you up if you happen to knock Von Balchow down.

'These fellows know just how to word a letter likely to appeal to the sporting instincts of poor boobs—like you!'

Biggles was hard to convince, but he finally allowed himself to be dissuaded. The following morning he did his usual patrol, which passed off without incident, and then returned, bored and bad-tempered, to the sheds, where he sat on an empty oil-drum and brooded over the matter of the previous day.

'What do those tadpoles think they're trying to do?' he asked Mahoney, who had seated himself on a chock* close by, as a large party of Oriental coolies** arrived and began unloading and spreading what appeared to be the brickwork of a house that had got in the way of a big shell.

'They're going to repair the road,' Mahoney told him.

'Who are those birds, anyway?' asked Biggles curiously.

'Chinese, from French Indo-China, I think. The French are using a lot of colonial troops, but most of them simply for fatigue work—road-making and so on—behind the Lines.'

'Is that their idea of making a road?' Biggles continued, as the coolies, after spreading a long line of

---

* Wooden blocks placed in front of an aircraft's wheels to prevent it moving before it is meant to.
** Workmen.

31

loose broken bricks, climbed back into a lorry and departed.

'Looks like it,' grinned Mahoney.

'A spot of steam-rollery wouldn't do any harm,' growled Biggles. 'We shall have to climb through those brickbats every time we go to or from the sheds to the mess.'

'It was a bad patch, anyway,' muttered Mahoney.

'Bad patch, my foot! We could get over it, anyway, but now we shall have to rope ourselves together and use alpenstocks and—Look out!'

He flung himself flat, as did Mahoney and his mechanics, who were fully alive to the danger that had precipitated itself from the clouds with a screaming roar. It was the green Boche two-seater. The pilot pulled up in a steep zoom at the bottom of his dive, and then tore off in the direction of the Lines. As he did so a small object, with a streamer attached, fell to the ground and bounced merrily over the aerodrome.

'It's Von Balchow!' yelled Biggles. 'Where's my blinkin' Camel? It's never ready when I want it! All right, flight-sergeant, don't start up—it isn't worth it; he's half-way back to the Lines by now. That's another message for little Jimmy, I'll bet. What does he say?'

Mahoney took the message from the air-mechanic who had retrieved it, tore open the envelope, read the contents, and then burst into a roar of laughter. 'Read it yourself!' he said.

Biggles read the message, which was in English, and his face grew slowly scarlet as he did so. 'The sausage-eating, square-headed son of a Bavarian offal-merchant!' he grated. 'He says he's sorry I didn't turn up, but he didn't really expect me; can he send me a packet of mustard to warm my feet? Warm my feet, eh? I'll warm his hog's-hide for him with my Vickers. Get my kite out, flight-sergeant!'

'Don't be a fool, Biggles!' cried Mahoney, becoming serious. 'Don't let him kid you into committing suicide.'

'You go and chew a bomb!' Biggles told him coldly. 'This is my show! I'm going to get that mackerel-faced merchant before the day is out, or I'll know the reason why. Let him bring his pals if he likes—the more the merrier. Mustard, eh?'

Mahoney shrugged his shoulders.

'I'll go and pack your kit,' he sneered, as Biggles climbed into his cockpit.

'You can pack what the dickens you like, but you let my kit alone,' Biggles told him wrathfully, as he took off.

He did not see Roland in the air, but he hardly expected to, so he made a bee-line for its aerodrome, of the whereabouts of which he was, of course, aware, having chased the Hun home the day before. He was evidently unexpected, for when he reached it the aerodrome was deserted, but a long row of Rolands on the tarmac suggested that the officers of the staffel were at home, so he announced his presence by zooming low over the mess, warming his guns as he did so, but disdaining to fire at the buildings or machines.

Instantly the scene became a hive of activity. The tarmac buzzed with running figures, some of whom sprang into the seats of the machines, while others spun the propellers. He picked out the green machine as he zoomed down the line, and from two thousand feet watched it taxi out ready to take off.

He knew that his best opportunity would come as the machine actually commenced its run across the aerodrome, but he refused to take any step that would enable Von Balchow's friends to say that he had taken an unfair advantage.

So he circled, waiting, until the machine was in the air at his own altitude before he launched his first attack, although he was well aware that other machines were climbing rapidly to get above him.

The Roland, with its powerful Mercedes engine, was a fighter of some renown, a two-seater comparable with our own Bristol fighter.* Biggles knew its qualities, for knowledge of the performance of one's adversary is the first rule of air fighting, so he was aware that his opponent would not be 'easy meat'. Still he felt curiously confident of the upshot.

Whatever else happened, he was going to get Von Balchow, the man who had suggested that he had cold feet! Afterwards he would deal with the others when the necessity arose.

He saw Von Balchow's gunner clamp a drum of ammunition on his mobile Parabellum** gun, and the pilot swing round to bring the gun to bear in preference to using his own fixed Spandau*** gun; but he was not to be caught thus.

Keeping the swirling propeller of the green machine between him and the deadly Parabellum, he went down in a fierce dive under the nose of the machine, zoomed up above and behind it, and before the gunner could swing his gun to bear, he fired a quick burst.

Then, while the gunner was tilting his gun upwards, he stood the Camel on its nose, went down in another

* Two-seater biplane fighter with remarkable manoeuvrability, in service 1917 onwards. It had one fixed Vickers gun for the pilot and one or two mobile Lewis guns for the observer/gunner.
** A mobile gun for the rear gunner usually mounted on a U-shaped rail to allow rapid movement with a wide arc of fire.
*** German machine guns were often called Spandaus, due to the fact that they were manufactured at Spandau in Germany.

dive, and came up under the other's elevators. He held his fire until a collision seemed inevitable, and then pressed the lever of his gun. It was only a short burst, but it was fired at deadly range.

Pieces flew off the green fuselage, and as he twisted upwards into a half roll Biggles noticed that the enemy gunner was no longer standing up.

'That's one of them!' he thought coolly. 'I've given them a bit out of their own copy-book.'

It was Richthofen*, the ace of German air-fighters and the great master of attack, who laid down the famous maxim 'when attacking two-seaters, kill the gunner first.'

Von Balchow, with his rear gun out of action, was crippled, and he showed little anxiety to proceed with the combat. Indeed, it may have been that he lost his nerve, for he committed the hopeless indiscretion of diving for his own aerodrome.

Biggles was behind him in a flash, shooting the green planes and struts** to pieces from a range that grew closer and closer as he pressed the control-stick forward. He could hear bullets ripping through his own machine, from the Rolands that had got above him, but he ignored them; the complete destruction of the green one was still uppermost in his mind.

Whether he actually killed the pilot or not he did not know, nor was he ever able to find out, although, in view of what occurred, it is probable that even if he was not killed by a bullet, Von Balchow must have been killed or badly injured in the crash.

* Manfred Von Richthofen 'the Red Baron'—German ace who shot down a total of 80 Allied aircraft. Killed in April 1918.
** 'Planes' refers to the wings of an aircraft, as well as referring to the whole structure. A biplane had four planes, two each side. Struts are the rigid supports between the fuselage and the wings of biplanes or triplanes.

Whether he was hit or not, the German had sufficient strength left to try to flatten out for a landing; but either he misjudged his distance or was mentally paralysed by the hail of lead that swept through his machine, for his wheels touched the ground while he was still travelling at terrific speed with his engine full on.

The Roland shot high into the air, somersaulted, and then buried itself in the ground in the most appalling crash that Biggles had ever seen. The victory could not have been more complete, for he had shot down his man on his own aerodrome!

As he turned away he saw the German mechanics race towards the wreck; then he turned his eyes upwards. Prepared as he was for something bad, his pardonable exultation received a rude shock when he saw that the air was alive with black-crossed machines, the gunners of which were making the most of their opportunity. To stay and fight them all was outside the question.

He had achieved what he had set out to do, and was more than satisfied; all that remained was to get home safely. So down he went and began racing in the direction of the Lines with his wheels just off the ground.

The pilots of the other machines were on his tail instantly, but their gunners, being unable to fire forward, could do nothing. Moreover, they had to act warily, for to overtake their mark meant diving into the ground. Nevertheless, Biggles did not remain on the same course for more than a few seconds at a time, but swerved from side to side, leaping over the obstructions like a steeplechaser.

More than one officer came home in the same way during the Great War; in fact, it was a recognised course of procedure in desperate circumstances, although in the case of a single-seater it had this disadvantage—the pilot had to accept the enemy's fire, without being able to return it.

Yet, although it went against the grain to run away, to stay and fight against such hopeless odds could only have one ending. Biggles knew it, and, forcing down the temptation to turn, he held on his way, twisting and turning like a snipe. More than one bullet hit the machine, yet no serious damage was done.

He shot across the back area enemy trenches, a mark for hundreds of rifles, yet he had done too much trench-strafing to be seriously concerned about them. All the same, he breathed a sigh of relief as he tore across the British lines to safety.

Then, as he sat back, limp from reaction, but satisfied that he had nothing more to fear, a shell, fired from a field gun, burst with a crash that nearly shattered his eardrums, and almost turned the Camel over. The engine kept going, but a cloud of smoke and hot oil spurted back over the windscreen from the engine, and he knew it had been damaged.

The revolution counter* began to swing back, and although he hung on long enough to get within sight of the aerodrome, he was finally forced to land, much to his disgust, in a convenient field about half a mile away.

The Camel finished its run about twenty yards from the hedge which bordered the road at that spot, and near where some Tommies** were working on an object which, as he climbed the gate, revealed itself to be a German tank—evidently one that had been captured or abandoned in the recent retreat.

He sat on the gate, watching it for a moment or two

* Used for counting revolutions per minute of the engine.
** Slang: British soldiers of the rank of Private.

37

while he removed his goggles and flying-coat, for the day was hot.

'Have any of you fellows got any water in your water-bottles?' he asked. 'My word, I am dry!'

'Yes, sir—here you are!' cried several of them willingly.

He accepted the first water-bottle, and smacked his lips with satisfaction after drinking a long draught.

'That's better!' he declared.

He watched the mechanics for a few minutes, for he was in no great hurry to return to the aerodrome, and after the recent brisk affair in the air he found it singularly pleasant to be sitting beside a country road. He decided that he would ask the first passer-by to leave word at the aerodrome as to where he was and how he was situated; the air-mechanics would then fetch the machine.

'What are you doing?' he asked the corporal who seemed to be in charge of the party, which he noticed was composed of Royal Engineers.

'The Huns left it behind in the retreat last week, sir,' replied the corporal. 'We were sent to fetch it back to the depot for examination, but she broke down, so we are trying to put her right.'

Biggles eyed the steel vehicle, with its ponderous caterpillar wheels, curiously.

'My word, I'd hate to be shut up in that thing!' he murmured.

'Oh, it's not so bad, sir. You come and look!' suggested the corporal. 'She stinks a bit of oil, but that's all!'

Biggles climbed off the gate and crawled through the small steel trap that opened in the rear end of the tank.

'By James, I should think she does stink!' he muttered. 'And it's hotter than hot!'

'You soon get used to that!' laughed the corporal.

'I suppose this is the wheel where the driver sits!' went on Biggles, climbing awkwardly into the small seat behind the wheel, and peering through the 'letter-box' slit that permitted a restricted view straight ahead.

'That's it, sir,' agreed the corporal. 'Excuse me a minute,' he went on as one of the men called something from outside.

Biggles nodded, and thumbed the controls gingerly. 'Well, I'd sooner have my own cockpit!' he mused, putting his foot on a pedal in the floor and depressing it absent-mindedly.

Instantly there was a loud explosion, and the machine jumped forward with a jolt that caused him to strike his head violently on an iron object behind him. At the same moment the door slammed to with a metallic clang.

# Chapter 4
# 'Stand clear — I'm coming!'

It was sheer instinct that made him clutch at the wheel and swing it round just as the front of the vehicle was about to take a tree head-on, but he managed to clear it and get back on to the road, down which he proceeded to charge at a speed that he thought utterly impossible for such a weight.

'Hi, corporal,' he shouted, 'come and stop the confounded thing! I can't!'

There was no reply, and, snatching a quick glance over his shoulder, he saw, to his horror, that the machine was empty.

'Great Scott! I'm sunk!' he muttered, white-faced.

Fortunately, the road was straight. But even so, it was only with difficulty that he was able to keep the tank on it, for the steel wheel vibrated horribly, and the steering-gear seemed to do strange things on its own. He eyed a distant bend in the road apprehensively.

'That's where I pile her up!' he thought. 'I shall never be able to make that turn. What a fool I was to get into this contraption!'

At that moment his eye fell on a throttle at his left side, and, forgetting that nearly all German controls worked in the opposite direction to our own, he, as he thought, pulled it back.

Immediately the machine bounded forward with renewed impetus, and the noise, which had been terrible enough before, became almost unbearable.

The bend in the road lurched sickeningly towards him, and, as he had prophesied, he failed to make it. He clutched at the side of the tank as it struck the bank and buried itself in the hedge. But he had forgotten the peculiar properties of this particular type of vehicle. Regarded as obstructions, the bank, ditch, and hedge were so trivial that the machine did not appear to notice them.

There was a whirring, slithering scream as the caterpillar wheels got a grip on the bank, and then, with a lurch like a sinking ship, it was over. The lurch flung him out of his seat, but he was back again at once, looking frantically for what lay ahead. A groan of despair broke from his lips when he saw that he was on his own aerodrome, heading straight for the sheds.

He snatched at the throttle, but could not move it, for it had slipped into the catch provided for it, and which prevented it from jarring loose with the vibration. But, naturally, he was unaware of this.

'Picture of an airman arriving home!' he muttered despairingly, as he tried to swerve clear of the hangars. 'Look out! Stand clear! I'm coming!' he bellowed, but his words were lost in the din.

But the air-mechanics who were on duty needed no warning. They rushed out of the hangars, and, after one glance at the terrifying apparition hurtling towards them, they bolted in all directions.

Biggles saw that a Camel plane—Mahoney's—stood directly in his path. He hung on to the wheel, but it was no use. The tank, which had seemed willing enough to turn when he was on the road, now refused to answer the controls in the slightest degree. The tank took the unlucky Camel in its stride, and Mahoney's pet machine disappeared in a cloud of flying fabric and splinters. Beyond it loomed the mouth of a hangar.

Mahoney rushed out of it, took one look at the mangled remains of his machine, and appeared to go mad.

'Look out, you fool—I can't stop!' screamed Biggles through the letter-box opening.

Whether Mahoney heard or not, Biggles did not know; but the flight-commander leapt for his life at the last moment, just as the tank roared past him and plunged into the entrance of the hangar. Where a bank and a hedge had failed to have any effect, it was not to be expected that a mere flimsy canvas hangar could stop it, and Biggles burst out of the far side like an express coming out of a tunnel, leaving a trail of destruction in his wake. The hangar looked as if a tornado had struck it.

An air-mechanic, who was having a quiet doze at the back of it, had the narrowest escape of his life. He woke abruptly, and sat up wonderingly as the din reached his ears, and then leapt like a frog as he saw death burst out through the structure behind him.

The tank's caterpillar wheels missed him by inches, and Biggles afterwards told him that he must have broken the world's record for the standing jump.

A party of men were under instruction in the concrete machine-gun pit a little further on. They heard the noise, but, mistaking it for a low-flying formation of planes, they did not immediately look round. They did so, however, as the steel monster plunged into it, and how they managed to escape being crushed to pulp was always a mystery to Biggles. The concrete pit was a tougher proposition than the tank had before encountered, and the tank gave its best. With a loud hiss of escaping steam, it gave one final convulsive lurch and then lay silent.

Biggles picked himself up from amongst the controls, and felt himself gingerly to see if any bones were

42

broken. A noise of shouting came from outside, so he crawled to the door and tried to unfasten it, but it refused to budge.

A strong smell of petrol reached his nostrils, and in something like a panic he hurled himself against the door, just as it was opened from the outside.

Blinking like an owl, with oil and perspiration running down his face, he sat up and looked about him stupidly.

Facing him was the C.O. Near him was Mahoney, and, close behind, most of the officers of the squadron, who had rushed up from the mess when they heard the crash. Biggles afterwards swore that it was the expressions on their faces that brought about his undoing. No one, he claimed, could look upon such comical amazement and keep a straight face.

Mahoney's face, in particular, appeared to be frozen into a stare of stunned incredulity. Whether it was that, or whether it was simply nervous reaction from shock, Biggles himself was unable to say, but the fact remains that he started to laugh. He got up and staggered to the corrugated iron wheel of his late conveyance and laughed until he sobbed weakly.

'These kites are too heavy on the controls!' he gurgled.

'So you think it's funny?' said a voice.

It held such a quality of icy bitterness that Biggles' laugh broke off short, and, looking up, he found himself staring into the frosty eyes of a senior officer, whose red tabs and red-rimmed cap betokened General Headquarters. Behind him stood a brigade-major and two aides-de-camp with an imposing array of red and gold on their uniforms. Close behind stood a Staff car, with a small Union Jack fixed to the radiator cap.

Biggles' mirth subsided as swiftly as a burst tyre,

and he sprang erect, for the expression on the face of the general spelt trouble.

The general lifted a monocle to his eye and regarded him 'like a piece of bad cheese,' as Biggles afterwards put it.

'What is the name of this—er—officer?' he asked Major Mullen, with a cutting emphasis on the word officer that made Biggles blush.

'Bigglesworth, sir.'

'I—' began Biggles, but the general cut him off.

'Silence!' he snapped in a voice that had been known to make senior officers tremble. 'Save your explanations for the court. You are under arrest!

'Please come with me, Major Mullen,' he went on, turning to the C.O. 'I should like a word with you.'

The C.O. cast one look at the culprit, in which reproach and pity were blended, and followed the general towards the squadron office.

Biggles' fellow-officers crowded round him in an excited, chattering group. Some thought the business a huge joke, and fired congratulations at him. Others, with visions of trouble ahead for Biggles, told him what a frightful ass he was, and wanted to know what made him do it. And one was frankly furious. That was Mahoney, whose machine had been smashed by the runaway tank.

Everybody was talking at once, and Biggles, thoroughly fed-up with the episode by this time, clapped his hands over his ears and endeavoured to push his way out of the crowd.

'No, you don't!' growled Mahoney, dragging him back. 'You've had your little joke, and now we want an explanation.'

'Joke?' spluttered Biggles. 'Joke, d'you call it?'

'Well, what else was it?' retorted Mahoney. 'Either

that or you've gone suddenly mad. Nobody but a madman or an idiot would go careering round in a tank smashing up things and endangering lives. Where in the name of suffering humanity did you get the thing?'

'I didn't get it—it got me! Do you think I wanted the confounded thing?' cried Biggles, exasperated.

Suddenly he threw off Mahoney's restraining hand and barged his way through the crowd towards the group of engineers approaching the tank.

'Hey, corporal!' he yelled. 'What d'you mean by shutting me up in that confounded thing and leaving me?'

'Wasn't my fault, sir,' replied the corporal. 'I was called out of the tank, and no sooner was I outside than you started it off. And the door slammed itself shut, sir.'

'Well, there's the very dickens to pay now!' said Biggles. 'The confounded thing ran away with me, and the steering went wrong. I've smashed up no end of property, and, to crown it all, I landed right at the feet of one of the big-wigs from Headquarters. You and I will be hearing a lot more about this, corporal, but I'll do my best to make things all right for you. After all, the fault's mine. I shouldn't have been so confoundedly curious and started monkeying about with the controls.

'Now,' he added, 'for goodness' sake buck up and take the perishing tank away. Sight of it gives me the shudders!'

'You'll shudder some more when the big-wigs have you up on the carpet,* my lad,' said Mahoney, who had been listening to the conversation. 'Take a bit of

---

* Slang: to be reprimanded

45

advice from me, and next time you want a joy-ride go in something less dangerous!'

'Joy-ride!' exclaimed Biggles. 'Perishing nightmare, you mean! Anyway,' he added bitterly, pointing, 'I have at least finished the perishing road for you!'

Where the heap of rubble had been ran a broad, flat track, like a well-made road. No steam-roller could have pressed those brickbats into the soft turf more thoroughly than had that runaway German tank!

# Chapter 5
# Biggles Gets a Bull

For four consecutive days the weather had been bad, and flying was held up. A thick layer of cloud, from which fell a steady drizzle of rain, lay over the trenches—and half Europe, for that matter—blotting out the landscape from the ground and from the air.

It is a well-known fact that when a number of people are thrown together in a confined space for a considerable period tempers are apt to become short and nerves frayed. Few of the officers of No. 266 Squadron were exceptions to that rule, and the atmosphere in the mess, due to the enforced inactivity, was becoming strained.

There was nothing to do. The gramophone had been played to a standstill, and playing-cards littered the tables, where they had been left by bridge-playing officers who had become tired of playing. One or two fellows were writing letters; the others were either lounging about or staring disconsolately through the window at the sullen, waterlogged aerodrome. The silence which had fallen was suddenly broken by Biggles, who declared his intention of going out.

'Are you going crazy, or something?' growled Mahoney, the flight-commander. 'You'll get wet through.'

'I can't help that,' retorted Biggles. 'I'm going out. If I don't go out I shall start gibbering like an ape in a cage.'

'You shouldn't find that very difficult,' murmured Mahoney softly.

47

Biggles glared, but said nothing. He left the room, slipping on his leather flying-coat and helmet in the hall, and opened the front door. Not until then did he realise just how foul the weather was, and he was half-inclined to withdraw his impetuous decision. However, more from a dislike of facing the others again in the ante-room than any other reason, he stepped out and splashed his way to the sheds.

The short walk was sufficient to damp his ardour, and he regarded the weather with increasing disfavour, that became a sort of sullen, impotent rage. It was ridiculous, and he knew it; but he could not help it. After twenty minutes pottering about the sheds he felt more irritable than he did when he had left the mess. He made up his mind suddenly.

'Get my machine out, flight-sergeant,' he snapped shortly.

'But, sir—'

'Did you hear what I said?'

'Sorry, sir!'

The machine was wheeled out and started up. Biggles took his goggles from his pocket and automatically put them over his helmet, but not over his eyes, for he knew that the rain would obscure them instantly; then he climbed into his seat.

'It's all right, I'm only going visiting,' he told the N.C.O. quietly. 'If anybody wants to know where I am, you can tell them I've gone over to No. 187 Squadron for an hour or two.'

'Very good, sir!' Flight-Sergeant Smyth watched him take-off with distinct disapproval.

Biggles found it was much worse in the air than he had expected. That is often the case. However bad conditions may seem on the ground, they nearly always appear to be far worse in the air. Still, by flying very low and hugging the road, he anticipated no difficulty in finding his destination. So, after sweeping back low over the sheds, he struck off in the direction of No. 187 Squadron's aerodrome at an altitude of rather less than one hundred feet, keeping an eye open for trees or other obstructions ahead.

Before five minutes had passed he was repenting his decision to fly, and inside ten minutes he was wondering what madness had come upon him that he should start on such an errand for no reason at all. Twice he overshot a bend in the road and had difficulty in finding it again.

The third time he lost it altogether, and, after tearing up and down with his wheels nearly touching the ground, during which time he stampeded a battery of horse-artillery* and caused a platoon of infantry to throw themselves flat in the mud, he knew that he was utterly and completely lost.

For a quarter of an hour or more he continued his crazy peregrinations, searching for some sign that would give him his bearings, and growing more and more angry, but in vain. Once he nearly collided with a row of poplars, and on another occasion nearly took the chimney-pot off a cottage.

It was the grey silhouette of a church tower that loomed up suddenly and flashed past his wing-tip that decided him to risk no more, but to come down and make inquiries about his position on the ground.

'I've had about enough of this!' he grunted as he throttled back and side-slipped down into a pasture. It was a praiseworthy effort to land in such extremely difficult conditions, and would have succeeded but for

* Horse-drawn artillery guns.

49

an unlooked-for but not altogether surprising circumstance.

Just as the machine was finishing its run, a dark object appeared in the gloom ahead, which at the last moment he recognised as an animal of the bovine species. Having no desire to run down an unoffending cow—both for his own benefit and that of the animal—he kicked out his foot and swerved violently—too violently.

There was a shuddering jar as the undercarriage slewed off sideways under the unaccustomed strain, and the machine slid to a standstill flat on the bottom of its fuselage, like a toboggan at the end of a run.

'Pretty good!' he muttered savagely, looking around for the cause of the accident, and noting with surprise that the animal had not moved its position.

Rather surprised, he watched it for a moment, wondering what it was doing; then he saw that it was tearing up clods of earth with its front feet, occasionally kneeling down to thrust at the ground with its horns.

An unpleasant sinking feeling took him in the pit of the stomach as he stared, now in alarm, at the ferocious-looking beast which, at that moment, as if to confirm his suspicions, gave vent to a low, savage bellow. He felt himself turn pale as he saw that the creature was a bull, and not one of the passive variety, either.

Bull-fighting was not included in his accomplishments. He looked around in panic for some place of retreat, but the only thing he could see was the all-enveloping mist and rain; what lay outside his range of vision, and how far away was the nearest hedge, he had no idea.

Then he remembered reading in a book that the sound of the human voice will quell the most savage beast, and it struck him that the moment was opportune to test the truth of this assertion. Never did an experiment fail more dismally. Hardly had he opened his lips when the bull, with a vicious snort, charged.

The cockpit of an aeroplane is designed to stand many stresses and strains, but a thrust from the horns of an infuriated bull is not one of them. And Biggles knew it. He knew that the flimsy canvas could no more withstand the impending onslaught than an egg could deflect the point of an automatic drill.

Just what the result would be he did not wait to see, for as the bull loomed up like an express train on one side of the machine, he evacuated the plane on the other.

# Chapter 6
# Lost in the Sky

It must be confessed that Biggles disliked physical exertion. In particular he disliked running, a not uncommon thing amongst airmen, who normally judge their speed in miles per minute rather than miles per hour. But on this occasion he covered the ground so fast that the turf seemed to fly under his feet.

Where he was going to he did not know, nor did he pause to speculate. His one idea at that moment was to put the greatest possible distance between himself and the aeroplane in the shortest space of time.

The direction he chose might have been worse; on the other hand, it might have been better. Had he gone a little more to the right he would have found it necessary to run a good quarter of a mile before he reached the hedge that bounded the field.

As it was, he only ran a hundred yards before he reached the boundary, which, unfortunately, at that point took the form of a barn by the side of which lay a shallow but extremely slimy pond.

Such was his speed that he only saw the barn, and the first indication he had of the presence of the pond was a clutching sensation around his ankles.

He came up in a panic, striking out madly, thinking that the bull had caught him. But, finding he could stand, for the water was not more than eighteen inches deep, he staggered to his feet and floundered to the far side. Having reached it safely he looked around for the bull, at the same time removing a trailing festoon of water-weed that hung around his neck like a warrior's laurel garland.

The animal was nowhere in sight, so after pondering the scene gloomily for a moment or two while he recovered his breath, Biggles made his way past the barn to a very dirty French farmyard.

There was no one about, so he continued on through a depressed-looking company of pigs and fowls to the farmhouse, which stood on the opposite side of the yard, and knocked on the door.

It was opened almost at once, and, somewhat to his surprise, by a remarkably pretty girl of seventeen or eighteen, who eyed him with astonishment. When he made his predicament known, in halting French, he was invited inside and introduced to her mother, who was busy with a cauldron by the fire.

Within a very short time he was sitting in front of the fire wrapped in an old overcoat, watching his uniform being dried on a clothes-line in front of it, and dipping pieces of new bread into a bowl of soup.

He felt some qualms about his machine, but he did not feel inclined to investigate, for he hesitated to lay himself open to ridicule by telling the others of his encounter with the bovine fury in the meadow.

'This,' he thought, as he stretched his feet towards the fire, 'is just what the doctor ordered! Much better than the mouldy mess!'

How long he would have remained is a matter for conjecture, for the fire was warm and he felt very disinclined to stir, but a sharp rat-tat at the door announced the arrival of what was to furnish the second half of his adventure that day.

Had he been watching the mademoiselle* he would

* French: miss, girl

have noted that she blushed slightly; but he was looking towards the door, so it was with distinct astonishment and no small disapproval that he watched the entrance of a very dapper French second-lieutenant, who wore the wings of the French Flying Corps on his breast.

The lieutenant, who was very young, stopped dead when he saw Biggles, while his brow grew dark with anger, and he shot a suspicious glance at mademoiselle, who hastened to explain the circumstances. The lieutenant, who, it transpired, was mademoiselle's fiancé, was mollified, but by no means happy at finding an English aviator in what he regarded as his own particular retreat, and he made it so apparent that Biggles felt slightly embarrassed.

However, they entered into conversation, and it appeared that the Frenchman was also in rather a difficult position. Three days previously he had set off from his escadrille* on an unofficial visit to his fiancée and had been caught by the weather.

When the time had come for him to leave, flying was absolutely out of the question, so he had to do what many other officers have had to do in similar circumstances. He rang up his squadron and told them that he had force-landed, but would return as soon as possible.

But, when the weather did not improve, he had been recalled. So, leaving his machine where he had landed it, which was in a field rather larger than the one Biggles had chosen, he had gone back to his aerodrome by road. Now, as the weather was reported to be improving and likely to clear before nightfall, he had been sent to fetch his machine.

Biggles, in turn, related how he had become lost in

* French: squadron.

54

the rain and had landed, with disastrous results to his undercarriage.

The lieutenant smiled in a superior way, as if getting lost was something outside the range of his imagination, and then crossed to the window to regard the weather, which was now certainly improving, but was by no means settled.

'I will fly you back to your squadron,' he declared.

Biggles started. The idea of being flown by anybody, much less a French second-lieutenant, left him cold, and he said as much.

But, as the afternoon wore on and the lieutenant's frown grew deeper, he began to understand the position. The Frenchman, who was evidently of a jealous disposition, was loath to leave him there with his best girl, yet he—the Frenchman—was due back at his squadron, and further delay might get him into trouble.

So, rather than cause any possible friction between the lovers, Biggles began seriously to contemplate the lieutenant's suggestion.

The weather was still dull, with low clouds scudding across the sky at a height of only two or three hundred feet. But it had stopped raining, and light patches in the clouds showed where they were thin enough for an aeroplane to get through.

In any case, Biggles knew that he would soon have to let Major Mullen, his commanding officer, know where he was, so, finally against his better judgment, he accepted the lieutenant's invitation—to the Frenchman's relief.

He thanked his hostesses for their hospitality, donned his uniform, and accompanied the pilot to a rather dilapidated Breguet plane, which stood dripping moisture in the corner of a field on the opposite side of the house from where he had left his Camel.

When his eyes fell on it he at once regretted his decision, but there was no going back. More than ever did he regret leaving the comfortable fireside as the Frenchman took off, with a stone-cold engine, in a steep climbing turn. A minute later they were swallowed up in the grey pall.

The period immediately following was a nightmare that Biggles could never afterwards recall without a shudder, for the Frenchman, quite lightheartedly, seemed to take every possible risk that presented itself. Finally, he staggered up through the clouds, levelled out above them, and set off on a course that Biggles was quite certain would never take them to Maranique.

'Hi, you're going too far east!' he yelled in the pilot's ear.

The Frenchman shrugged his shoulders expressively.

'Who flies? Me or you?' he roared.

Biggles' lips set in a straight line.

'This isn't going to be funny!' he muttered. 'This fool will unload me the wrong side of the Lines if I don't watch him!' He could see the lieutenant's lips moving; he was evidently singing to himself, as he flew, with the utmost unconcern.

Biggles' lips also moved, but he was not singing.

'Hi,' he shouted again presently, 'where the dickens are you going?'

The Frenchman looked surprised and pained.

'Maranique, you said, did you not?' he shouted.

'Yes. But it's that way!' cried Biggles desperately, pointing to the north-west.

'No—no!' declared the Frenchman emphatically.

Biggles felt like striking him, but that course was inadvisable as there was no dual control-stick in his cockpit. So all he could do was to sit still and fume, deploring the folly that had led him into such a fix.

56

Meanwhile, the Frenchman continued to explore the sky in all directions, until even Biggles had not the remotest idea of their position.

'We only need to barge into a Hun,' he thought, 'and that'll be the end! I'll choke this blighter when I get him on the ground!'

The lieutenant, who evidently had his own methods of navigation, suddenly throttled back, and, turning with a smile, pointed downwards.

'Maranique!' he called cheerfully.

'Maranique, my foot!' growled Biggles, knowing quite well that they could not be within twenty miles of it.

The Frenchman, without any more ado, plunged downwards into the grey cloud.

Biggles turned white and clutched at the sides of the cockpit, prepared for the worst. There was no altimeter in his cockpit, and he fully expected the Frenchman to dive straight into the ground at any second. To his infinite relief, not to say astonishment, they came out at about two hundred feet over an aerodrome.

It was not Maranique. But Biggles did not mind that. He was prepared to land anywhere, and be thankful for the opportunity, even if it meant walking home. The Frenchman's idea of flying, he decided, was not his.

It was nearly dark when they touched their wheels on the soaking turf near the edge of the aerodrome. In fact, they were rather too near, for the machine finished its run with its nose in a ditch and its tail cocked high in the air.

Biggles evacuated the machine almost as quickly as he had left his own Camel plane when the bull had charged, and, once clear, surveyed the wreck dispassionately.

57

'Thank goodness he did it, and not me!' was his mental note.

His attention was suddenly attracted by the curious antics of the Frenchman, who, with a cry of horror, had leapt to the ground and was fumbling with a pistol.

For a moment Biggles did not understand, and thought the wretched fellow was going to shoot himself, out of remorse. But then Biggles saw that he was mistaken.

'What's wrong?' he asked.

'Voilà!*' The lieutenant pointed, and, following the outstretched finger, Biggles turned ice-cold with shock. Dimly through the darkening mist, not a hundred yards away, stood an aeroplane.

It did not need a large cross on the side of its fuselage to establish its identity. The machine, beyond all doubt and question, was a German Rumpler** plane!

Biggles turned to the wretched Frenchman in savage fury.

'You blithering lunatic!' he snarled. 'I told you you were too far to the east. Look where you've landed us!'

The lieutenant paid no attention, for he was busy performing the last rites over his machine. He raised the pistol, and at point blank range sent a shot into the petrol-tank. Instantly the machine was a blazing inferno.

Then, side by side, they ran for their lives. They heard shouts behind them, but they did not stop.

They ran until they reached a wood, into which they plunged, panting for breath, and then paused to consider the position, which was just about as unpleasant as it could be. The place was dripping with moisture, and Biggles' teeth were chattering, for his

* French: There!
** German two-seater biplane for observation and light bombing raids.

uniform was by no means dry when he had put it on at the farmhouse.

But there was nothing, apparently, that they could do, so they pressed on into the heart of the wood, where they crouched until it was dark, hardly speaking a word, with Biggles furious and the Frenchman 'desolated' almost to the point of suicide.

Then, with one accord, they crept from their hiding-place towards the edge of the wood, coming out in a narrow, deserted lane.

Suddenly the Frenchman clutched Biggles' arm, his eyes blazing.

'The Rumpler!' he hissed. 'We will take the Rumpler, and I will yet fly you back to Maranique!'

Biggles started, for the idea had not occurred to him, and he eyed his companion with a new respect and admiration. He had no intention of letting the Frenchman fly him to Maranique—or anywhere else—but if they could manage to get control of that machine they might yet escape, and even reach home that night. It was a project that many prisoners of war, and flying officers at large in hostile territory, dreamt of.

'Come on! We'll try, anyway!' Biggles said crisply, and set off in the direction of the aerodrome. It was nervy work, and more than once they had to crouch shivering in the bottom of a ditch, or in soaking undergrowth, while bodies of men moved towards the Lines, or backward to the rest camps. As it so happened, none came anywhere near them.

With the stealth of Red Indians on the warpath, they crept towards their objective. In his heart Biggles felt certain that by this time the machine would have been put in a hangar, from which it would be impossible to extract it without attracting attention. If that was so, it was the end of the matter.

59

As they slowly neared the spot where they had last seen the German machine a low murmur of voices reached them from the direction of the Frenchman's crashed Breguet, and once Biggles thought he heard a laugh. The crash, it seemed, was amusing.

Well, maybe he would have laughed had the situation been reversed. But as it was, there was little enough to raise a smile as far as they were concerned.

Hoping all the officers of the German squadron had collected round the crash, they made a wide detour to avoid it, and presently came upon the Rumpler almost in the same position as they had last seen it.

Someone had moved it slightly nearer the sheds—that was all. What was even more important, not a soul was in sight.

Now that the moment for action had arrived, Biggles felt curiously calm; the Frenchman, on the other hand, was panting with excitement.

'You start the prop; I will open the throttle!' he breathed.

'Not on your life!' declared Biggles. 'I'll do the pouring. I've done all the flying I'm going to with you. You make for the prop when I say the word "go".'

The Frenchman was inclined to argue, but Biggles clenched his fists, with the desired result, so he took a final look round and crouched for the spring.

'Go!' he snapped.

Together they burst from cover and dashed towards the solitary machine. Biggles, as arranged, made for the cockpit, while the French lieutenant tore round the wing to the prop. Even as he put his foot into the stirrup to climb up Biggles staggered backwards; his heart seemed to stop beating. A head had appeared above the rim of the cockpit. He stared, but there was no doubt about it—a man was sitting in the machine.

The French pilot saw him, too, for a groan burst from his lips.

Then a voice spoke. It was not so much what the man said, or the tone of voice he employed, that struck Biggles all of a heap. It was the language he used. It was English—perfect English.

'What the dickens do you two fellows think you're going to do?' he said as he stood up and then jumped to the ground.

Biggles' jaw sagged as he stared at an officer in the Royal Flying Corps uniform. 'Who—who are you?' he gasped.

'Lynsdale's my name—No. 281 Squadron. Why?'

Biggles began to shake.

'Who does this kite belong to?' he asked, pointing to the Rumpler.

'Me. At least, I reckon it's mine. I forced it to land this morning, and we towed it in this afternoon.'

'What aerodrome is this?' Biggles queried shakily.

'St. Marie Fleur. No. 281 Squadron moved in about a week ago. As a matter of fact, we've only got one Flight here so far, but the others are expected any day. By the way,' Lynsdale went on, turning to the Frenchman, 'are you by any chance the johnnie who landed here about an hour ago and set fire to his kite?'

But the Frenchman was not listening. He had burst into tears and was sitting on the wheel of the Rumpler, sobbing.

'Never mind, cheer up, old chap!' said Biggles kindly. 'There's plenty more where that one came from, and we're better off than we thought we were, anyway.'

'You'd both better come up to the mess and have some grub, while I ring up your people and tell them you're here!' observed Lynsdale, trying hard not to laugh.

# Chapter 7
# The Human Railway

One of the most characteristic features of flying during the Great War was the manner in which humour and tragedy so often went hand in hand. At noon a practical joke might set the officers' mess rocking with mirth; by sunset, or perhaps within the hour, the perpetrator of it would be gone for ever, fallen to an unmarked grave in the shellholes of No Man's Land.

Laughter, spontaneous and unaffected, with Old Man Death watching, waiting, ever ready to strike.

Those whose task it was to clear the sky of enemy aircraft knew it, but it did not worry them. They seldom alluded to it. When it thrust itself upon their notice they forgot it as quickly as they could. It was the only way.

That attitude in mind, that philosophy of life in warfare, was aptly instanced by the events of a certain summer day in the history of No. 266 Squadron.

The day was hot. The morning patrol had just returned, and the officers of 266 Squadron were lounging languidly in the ante-room, with cooling drinks at their elbows. Maclaren, who had led the patrol, his flying suit thrown open down the front, exposing the blue silk pyjamas in which he had been flying, leaned against the mantelpiece, a foaming jug in his right hand. He was using his left to demonstrate the tactics of the Hun who had so nearly got him, and he punctuated his narrative by taking mighty draughts of the contents of the jug, which he himself had concocted.

'He turned, and I turned,' he continued, 'and I had him stone cold in my sights. I grabbed for my gun lever'—his forehead wrinkled into a grimace of disgust—'and my guns packed up. Well, it wasn't their fault,' he continued disconsolately, 'there was nothing in 'em! It was the first time in my life that I've run out of ammunition without knowing it!

'Luckily for me, the Hun had had enough and pushed off, or I shouldn't be here now. He's probably still wondering why I didn't go after him. I don't suppose he'll ever know how mighty thankful I was to see him go, and I don't mind telling you I wasted no time in getting home. It was a red machine—an Albatross—so it may have been Richthofen himself. He certainly could fly.

'A dozen times I thought I'd got him, but before I could shoot he'd gone out of my sights. Two or three times while I was looking for him he had a crack at me. I've got an idea I've been rather lucky. I—'

He broke off, and all eyes turned towards the swing-doors that led into the dining-room as they were pushed open and a stranger entered.

He did not enter as one would expect a new officer joining a squadron to enter. There was nothing deferential or even in the slightest degree respectful about his manner.

Indeed, so unusual was his method of entry upon the scene that the amazed occupants of the room could only stare wonderingly. Actually, what he did was to fling the doors open wide, and, holding them open with outstretched arms, cry in a shrill Cockney voice: 'Passing Down Street and Hyde Park Corner!' He then emitted a series of sounds that formed an excellent imitation of a Tube train starting, punctuated with the usual clanging of doors.

The rumble of the departing 'train' died away and the stranger advanced smiling into the room. Half-way across it he stopped, waved his handkerchief like a guard's flag, whistled shrilly, and called: 'Any more for Esher, Walton, Weybridge, Byfleet or Woking?'

Then he sat down at a card table opposite Biggles. But the performance was not yet finished, as the spellbound watchers were to discover.

'Two to Waterloo!' he cried sharply. He followed this instantly by bringing down his elbow sharply on the table, at the same time letting his fist fall forward so that his knuckles also struck the table. The noise produced, which can only be described as 'clonk, clonker, clonk, clonk-er', was precisely the sound made in a railway booking-office used for punching the date on tickets issued.

Having completed these items from his repertoire, he sat back with a smile and awaited the applause he evidently expected. There was, in fact, a general titter, for the imitations had been excellent and admirably executed.

Biggles, whose nerves were a bit on edge, did not join in, however. He was tired, and the sudden disturbance irritated him. He merely stared at the round, laughing face in front of him with faint surprise and disapproval.

'What do you think you are—a railway?' he asked coldly.

The other nodded.

'I'm not always a railway, though. Sometimes I'm an aeroplane,' he observed seriously.

'Is that so?' replied the astonished Biggles slowly.

Another titter ran round the room, and the stranger rose.

'Yes,' he said. 'Sometimes I'm a Camel.'

'A Camel!' gasped Biggles incredulously.

The other nodded.

'I can do any sort of aeroplane I like, with any number of engines, but I like being a Camel best. Watch me!' Forthwith he gave a brilliant sound imitation of a Camel being started up.

With vibrating lips producing the hum of a rotary engine, he ran round the room with his arms—which were evidently intended to be the planes of the machine—outstretched. He 'landed' neatly in an open space, and then 'taxied' realistically back to his seat.

As the 'engines' backfired and then died away with a final swish-swoosh, there was a shout of laughter, in which Biggles was compelled to join.

'Pretty good!' he admitted. 'What's your name, by the way?'

'Forbes, Clarence. Born 1894. Occupation, invent—'

'All right. Cut out the rough stuff,' interrupted Biggles. 'You won't mind my saying that it is my considered opinion that you are slightly off your rocker!'

The other raised his eyebrows.

'Slightly! My dear young sir,' he protested, 'you do me less than justice. Most people are firmly convinced that I am absolutely barmy. They call me the Mad Hatter.'

'They're probably right!' admitted Biggles. 'We shall probably think the same when we know you better. Did you say you were an inventor?'

Forbes nodded.

'Sh!' he whispered, glancing around with mock furtiveness. 'Spies may be listening. Presently I will show you some of the inventions I have produced in readiness for my debut in a service squadron.'

Biggles started.

'Don't you start messing about with our machines!' he said, frowning.

Forbes looked pained.

'I wouldn't dream of doing such a thing!' he declared. 'But wait until you have seen—'

'Is Mr Forbes here, please?' called a mess waiter from the door.

Forbes looked round.

'Yes, what is it?' he asked.

'The C.O. wants to see you in the office, sir!'

'I'm on my way,' replied Forbes rising. Emitting an unbelievable volume of sound that could be recognised as a misfiring two-stroke motor-cycle, he steered himself to the door and disappeared.

'Mad as a hatter! He said it, and, by James, he's right!' said Biggles. 'If he goes on like that on the ground, just think what he must be like in the air! I should say the formation that gets the job of trailing him about the sky is in for a thin time.'

The orderly appeared again.

'Mr Bigglesworth, please, wanted on the telephone!' he called.

Biggles hurried from the room. Three minutes later he returned and resumed his seat. There was a curious expression on his face. He looked up, and his eyes caught those of Mahoney, the flight-commander.

'Have you been awarded the V.C., or something?' asked the flight-commander curiously.

'No, but I shall deserve it by tonight, if I live to see it,' muttered Biggles morosely.

'Why, what's doing?'

'The C.O. says I'm to show Forbes the Line—this afternoon!' The shout of laughter that went up could be heard on the far side of the aerodrome.

# Chapter 8
# Orange Fire!

When Biggles went up to the shed after lunch he found Forbes already there awaiting his arrival. The new man, who had evidently been making some adjustments to his machine, for his hands were filthy, accosted him eagerly.

'Come and have a look at my new device for keeping Huns off my tail,' he invited. 'You'll be sorry for the Hun who gets behind me—and so will he!'

'No, thanks! Personally, I prefer to stick to my Vickers guns to deal with Huns. And it isn't my fault if they're behind me,' Biggles said meaningly. 'In 266 Squadron, when we see Huns we go for them.'

'I see,' replied the other coolly, not in the least put out. 'Then you don't want to see—'

'No, thanks,' said Biggles again. 'I think I shall be able to manage with my guns, and I advise you to do the same.'

'Just as you like.'

'All you have to do this afternoon,' went on Biggles, 'is to keep your eye on me. Stick close, and try to pick up as many landmarks as you can. We'll go as far as the Line and fly along it for a bit, but I don't expect we shall actually go over. In any case, keep close to me whatever happens.'

Forbes nodded.

'I will,' he said seriously.

Five minutes later they were in the air, climbing in wide circles in the direction of the Front Line. From time to time Biggles tilted a wing* and pointed to some outstanding landmark—a lake, a mine crater, a clump of shell-blasted tree trunks that had once been a wood, or a river, noting with satisfaction that the pilot he was escorting flew well, and what was more important, kept his place even in spite of the usual burst of archie that greeted them.

For an hour or more they flew, following a definite course and climbing to a great height above the Lines.

Biggles, who never lost an opportunity of picking up useful information, was trying to locate an enemy archie battery that had been annoying them persistently with remarkably accurate shooting, when he was startled by Forbes, who suddenly drew up level with him, and who, having attracted his attention, pointed.

Biggles, following the outstretched finger, saw a small grey speck fleeting across the face of the sun. Mentally congratulating the beginner on his watchfulness and 'spotting' ability, Biggles turned his nose in the direction of the distant machine, at the same time subjecting the sky around to a searching scrutiny.

Was it a trap? He did not know, but his eyes probed the atmosphere anxiously in order to try to find out. He had no wish to be caught in an awkward predicament with the responsibility of a new man on his hands. The two Camels were flying at fourteen thousand feet, while the other, which Biggles now saw was an Aviatik**—a German plane—was a good two thousand feet above them, and making for home.

He watched it for a moment or two undecided, then, concluding that pursuit was not worthwhile, he would

* No planes had radios at the time so messages between pilots were conveyed by hand or plane movements.
** German armed reconnaissance biplane with one fixed machine gun for the pilot and a mobile gun for the observer/gunner.

have turned away, for they had already crossed the Lines.

But this evidently did not suit Forbes, who protested violently with much hand-waving from his cockpit.

Rightly or wrongly, Biggles always blamed himself for what followed, for he was the leader, and had he turned, Forbes would, or should, have followed him. But the new man's enthusiasm spoilt Biggles' better judgment, and after a good look around to make sure that the sky was clear, he held on after the Boche two-seater.

Frankly, he did not expect to catch it, but it was good practice, and provided they did not go too far over the Line they could take no harm.

It was unfortunate that Forbes, in his anxiety to overtake the enemy two-seater should 'overshoot' his leader at the very moment that Biggles' engine began to give trouble. At first it was only a very faint knock, but it was sufficient to bring a frown to his face. The rev-counter was already falling back.

It was now Biggles' turn to try to catch Forbes, to signal to him that he could not go on. But his pupil's eyes were fixed intently on the grey silhouette ahead, and not once did he look in his leader's direction.

Biggles fumed, but in vain. He was only twenty or thirty yards behind, but both machines were flying on full throttle, and he had no reserve of speed to overtake the other. The knocking in the engine grew steadily worse.

'This is no use—I shall have to get back,' he decided savagely. 'Forbes will have to take his luck.' He eased back the throttle to take the strain off the engine, and swung round in the direction of the Lines, now some miles away.

Once he had turned, the distance between the two

Camels increased at alarming speed, but he watched the other as long as he could, and it may have been due to that fact that he failed to notice what normally he would have seen.

To his infinite relief, he saw Forbes turn and come racing after him. Satisfied, he looked down, and then saw with uneasiness, from the shell-smoke on the ground, that the wind had freshened. Still, he was not alarmed, for he had plenty of height to reach the Lines, even in a glide without his engine. Then he began his systematic searching of the sky.

He did not look very long. Sweeping down the Lines, not more than a mile away, was a ragged formation of torpedo-shaped aeroplanes. There was no need to look twice—they were Albatrosses; and that the enemy planes had seen him and were racing to cut him off was as clear as daylight.

His heart grew cold as he watched them—not for himself, but for Forbes, who was still trailing along a couple of miles behind. Bitterly Biggles repented his folly in allowing himself to be persuaded so far over the Lines with an untried beginner.

He toyed with his throttle to try to squeeze a few more revs out of the engine, but it grew worse instead of better.

What should he do? To wait for Forbes in such circumstances was sheer suicide, and even if he did wait there was little he could do. He hoped and prayed that Forbes would see the danger and turn off at a tangent, in which case Forbes might just beat the Huns to the Lines, if they stopped to deal with him— Biggles—first.

But either Forbes did not see or he was made of sterner stuff, for straight as an arrow he held his machine towards the approaching storm. As a last resort Biggles deliberately turned towards the Huns, thinking that perhaps Forbes, who would be watching him, would then be certain to see them; but it was no use. In fact, it only made matters worse, for Forbes merely turned to follow him straight into the lion's mouth, so to speak.

Biggles' lips became a bloodless line.

'Well, if he's going to follow me whatever I do, I might as well make a dash for it!' he thought. And, swinging round straight in the direction of the Lines, now about two miles away, he shoved the control-stick forward savagely.

His engine revs had fallen practically to zero, so there was no question of staying to fight. Looking back over his shoulder, he saw Forbes turn again to follow him, and in that order they raced for safety.

First came Biggles, now down to about five thousand feet; then Forbes, still about half a mile behind; then came the Hun formation, a dozen or more of them, like a pack of hungry wolves.

The Lines leapt up towards them, but the Huns, who by this time may have seen Biggles' slowly revolving propeller, had no intention of letting such an easy prey escape.

Standing nearly on their shark-like noses, tails cocked high in the air, the enemy planes thundered down, and the distance closed between them and their quarry.

Biggles, flying with his head twisted round over his shoulder, saw that the Albatrosses would catch Forbes first, as indeed they must, and he gritted his teeth in impotent fury at his own helplessness.

They actually reached the Lines as the shooting began, and the rattle of the guns came faintly to his ears. He stared, with a curious tightening of the muscles

71

of his face, as Forbes' machine swerved as if it had been hit; but he recovered and swung round on the original course immediately behind him.

Its nose went down into a steeper dive until it was no more than a hundred yards behind him. The Huns closed up.

'Now they've got him!' he thought, for the Camel was flying in a straight line with the whole pack behind it. 'Why doesn't the young fool turn, loop, half-roll, spin—anything rather than sit still and be shot like a sitting rabbit?' He quivered. Never had he felt so utterly useless.

'Perhaps the fellow's waiting for me to do something,' thought Biggles—'waiting for me to turn on the Huns and give him a lead! And I can't do a blessed thing!'

The knowledge that Forbes would think he—Biggles—was running away, leaving him to his fate, brought a scarlet flush to his cheeks. Forbes could not know that his engine had packed up.

Well, there was nothing he could do so he braced himself for the worst. Instead, he saw the most amazing spectacle that it had ever been his lot to witness.

As the Huns closed in to deliver the knock-out blow a streak of orange fire, followed by a cloud of smoke, spurted backwards from the Camel. What it was he did not know. At first he thought that Forbes' machine was on fire, but as a second streamer of fire leapt backwards he saw that it was not so. Spellbound, he could only watch.

At the appearance of the first fiery missile the Huns had swerved wildly, as indeed they had every reason to, and the thing actually passed between the planes of the leading Albatross. It also went very close to one of those in the rear.

At the appearance of the second one there was gen-

eral confusion as each pilot tried to avoid it. In the
melée the wings of two of them became locked. For
perhaps five seconds they clung together. Then they
broke away, and shedding woodwork and fabric,
plunged downwards, spinning.

Biggles watched speechlessly, unable to understand
what was happening, conscious only that two of the
enemy machines had gone—a fact that filled him with
intense exultation.

Two more streamers of fire and smoke hurtled aft
from Forbes' machine; they went wide, but they served
their purpose. The Albatrosses had had enough. The
enemy formation scattered as the machines pulled out
in all directions, and although they hung about in the
vicinity, presumably to watch the fire-spitting phenom-
enon, they gave up the pursuit.

Biggles gave a heartfelt sigh of relief, hardly daring
to believe that escape was now practically an
accomplished fact. His brain became normal, and into
his mind for the first time crept snatches of the conversation on the tarmac before they had begun the fight.
What was it Forbes had said? 'Come and see my
device,' and 'You'll be sorry for the Hun who gets on
my tail!'

That must have been the device he had seen working,
but what on earth was it? It looked as if it might have
been a glorified Very* pistol, attached to some part of
the machine, trained to fire backwards and operated
from the cockpit. But how the dickens did Forbes reload
it? It was too big for a Very light, anyway.

'Well, it's a problem that will have to wait for an
answer,' Biggles decided. 'It's no use guessing!'

* A short-barrelled pistol for firing coloured flares for signalling. Before
the days of radios in planes, coloured flares were often used to convey
messages.

73

The chief thing now was to get on the ground without cracking up, for his engine was too far gone for him to hope to get back to the aerodrome, so he looked about anxiously for a suitable place to set the machine down.

He picked out a field, small, and by no means even-surfaced, and was about to side-slip down towards it when he became aware that Forbes' machine was acting in a very curious manner.

The engine had been cut off, and it seemed to be slipping from left to right. Once it very nearly stalled, but the pilot caught it in the very nick of time.

Biggles watched, with his heart in his mouth, only too well aware that something was wrong, as the Camel shot past him, steering a zigzag course for the same field in which he himself had proposed to land.

He half expected Forbes to make some signal as he passed, but he did not. With head erect, sitting bolt upright in the cockpit, Forbes seemed to be staring fixedly at something that lay directly ahead. In that direction the Camel flew straight towards the ground.

Somehow Biggles knew just what was going to happen. Out of the corner of his eyes, as he slipped in over the hedge of the field, he saw the other machine half flatten out, but too late. The wheels and under-carriage were swept off in a cloud of dust; the Camel bounced high into the air, and then drove nose first into the ground.

Biggles landed, and without waiting for his machine to finish its run, he leaped out and sprawled headlong; but he was on his feet in an instant, running like a madman towards the crash. A little wisp of smoke was drifting sluggishly into the air from the engine, and he grew cold at the thought of what it portended.

Fire! The smoke was petrol vapour, caused by petrol from the smashed tanks running over the hot cylinders of the engine. But the dreaded horror had not occurred when he reached the machine. The pilot was still strapped in his seat, in a crumpled position.

Troops were running up from all directions, for they had come down in the middle of the support Lines.

'Here! Quick!' panted Biggles, as he strove to force aside a flying-wire* that was holding the pilot in his seat.

He knew that the danger of fire was by no means past; one dying spark from the magneto,** and the petrol-soaked wreckage would go up like gunpowder. He had seen it happen before.

'Now then—all together—steady—that's right—steady!' he cried, as new hands came to the rescue and between them released the unconscious pilot and laid him on the grass.

Forbes opened his eyes and Biggles' hands ran questioningly over him, searching for what he hoped he would not find—the damp, sticky patch over a bullet that had found a billet.

'Where did they get you, laddie?' he asked, for he felt certain that Forbes had been hit.

The wounded man blinked, and his eyes sought those of his leader.

'Got me through both legs,' he breathed. 'That blood on my face is coming from my nose; I think I busted it on the stubs of my guns when I crashed.'

Biggles nodded sympathetically, relieved to find that the damage was no worse. A party of R.A.M.C.***

---

* Flying wires—particularly on biplane aircraft—help to hold the wings in position in the air. Landing wires have the weight of the wings when the aircraft is on the ground.
** A generator producing a spark which fires the engine.
*** Royal Army Medical Corps.

men arrived at the double; iodine and field dressings were produced and first-aid applied.

'You'll be O.K.,' Biggles said, when he saw the wounds were not serious. 'You fainted from loss of blood, I expect.'

Forbes nodded weakly.

'Yes,' he muttered, 'I felt myself going—that was the rotten part of it. I knew I was going to crash. My legs wouldn't work; I couldn't keep 'em on the rudder-bar, so the kite was slipping about all over the place. They got me first burst, confound it!'

'Why on earth didn't you push off when you saw that bunch,' said Biggles, 'and try to get home on your own, instead of trailing along after me? All the same, it was a stout effort. They'd have got me if you hadn't done what you did.'

'Rot! I wasn't thinking about you, anyway!' declared Forbes, with a whimsical smile.

'No-o?'

'No. I wanted to try out my apparatus, but the Huns were a bit too quick for me.'

'What the dickens was it?' Biggles demanded.

'Rockets. You know the rockets they used to use for balloon strafing?'

'Of course!' he replied.

'Well, I've made a gadget to hold 'em on—backwards,' Forbes explained. 'When they go off, they shoot behind me. My idea was to surprise a Hun who got on my tail—give him something he wasn't expecting.

'I wanted to show it to you before we started, but you wouldn't look. I'll explain it to you when I come back from hospital.'

'Fine!' exclaimed Biggles. 'Fine!'

A motor-ambulance trundled up, and Forbes was lifted inside. Biggles gripped his hand.

'Cheerio, kid!' he said. 'I'll tell the Old Man you put up a great show!'

'Thanks!' returned Forbes. His elbow came down smartly on the side of the vehicle, his fist followed it. The ambulance driver looked round in surprise at the sound—clonk, clonk-er, clonk, clonk-er!

'What was that?' he asked.

'Two to Waterloo!' grinned Forbes.

# Chapter 9
# Out for Records!

The greatest number of enemy aeroplanes to fall in one day during the Great War under the guns of any single airman numbered six. At the end of the War two or three officers had accomplished this amazing record, which was first established by Captain J. L. Trollope shortly before he himself was shot down.

Biggles' record day's bag was four. On one occasion he shot down three enemy planes before breakfast, and with this flying start, so to speak, he thought he stood a good chance of beating his own record. But it came to nothing. He roved the sky for the rest of that day, until he nearly fell asleep in the cockpit, without seeing a single Hun.

Disgusted, he went back to his aerodrome at Maranique, and to bed. So four remained his limit, and each one was a well-deserved success.

The affair in which he had got three victories before breakfast was simple by comparison. It came about this way:

Whilst on a dawn patrol he saw a formation of five enemy scouts, and he attacked immediately 'out of the sun'—without being seen. He swooped down on the rear of the formation and picked off a straggler without the others even noticing it. Shifting his nose slightly, he brought his sights to bear on the next machine, and killed the pilot with a burst of five rounds.

The second machine was spinning downwards before

the first had reached the ground, so he had two falling machines in the air at once.

The remaining three machines heard the shooting, however, and, turning, came back at the daring British scout. Barely touching his controls, Biggles took the leader in his sights, head-on, and succeeded in setting fire to it with his first burst! For a matter of twenty rounds he had secured three victories, all within the space of two minutes.

The surviving members of the enemy formation dived for cover and took refuge in a cloud before he could come up with them. And, as I have said, he did not see another enemy machine for the rest of that day.

The occasion on which he scored four successes was a very different proposition, and not without a certain amount of humour, although it must be admitted that only three of these victories were confirmed.

The anti-aircraft gunners put in a claim for the last one, and although Biggles was quite satisfied in his own mind that he shot it down, the subsequent court of inquiry, for reasons best known to themselves, gave the verdict to the gunners.

It happened shortly after Captain Trollope had astonished all the squadrons in France by his amazing exploit. Nothing else was talked about in the officers' mess of Squadron No. 266 one guest night, when, amongst others, Captain Wilkinson and several pilots of Squadron No. 287 were present.

Wilkinson, better known as Wilks, had taken the view that although the feat was difficult, it was really surprising that it had not been done before, considering the number of combats that took place daily. At the same time, he claimed, perhaps correctly, that there was a certain amount of luck in it.

One could not, he asserted, take on a formation of

six or more Huns and hope to bring them all down; that was asking too much. Yet to find six isolated machines in quick succession, in days when machines were flying more and more in formation, was also expecting rather a lot.

Again, the combats would have to take place near the Line, within view of the artillery observers, or confirmation would be impossible. The other method of obtaining confirmation—from an eyewitness in the air—might lead to some doubt as to who had actually shot down the machine, as it was more than likely that both of them would be engaged in the combat.

The upshot of the whole matter was that before the evening was out the affair had assumed a personal note, the members of each squadron represented at dinner each declaring that their particular squadron would be the next to do the trick—and perhaps beat it.

Wilks in particular was convinced that if the double 'hat trick' was to be done again, the S.E.5's* of Squadron No. 287 would be the machines to do it.

In Biggles' opinion, a Camel of Squadron No. 266 was more likely to win the honour.

This was, of course, merely friendly rivalry, each pilot naturally supporting his own squadron and the type of machine which he himself flew. There the matter ended when the party broke up, and no one expected that any more would be heard of it.

But before the stars had completely disappeared from the sky next morning, Mannering, the recording officer of Squadron No. 287, informed Wat Tyler, the recording officer of Squadron No. 266, by telephone, that Captain Wilkinson had already shot down three machines. What was more, he had had them confirmed,

* Scouting experimental single-seater British biplane fighter in service 1917–1920, fitted with two or three machine guns.

and at that moment he was in the air again looking for more.

This information was quickly conveyed to the flight-commanders and pilots of Squadron No. 266. Biggles, who was still in bed, heard the news with incredulity and chagrin.

'Great Scotland Yard, Tyler!' he cried. 'We can't let Squadron No. 287 get away with this! If Wilks knocks down any more machines today we shall never hear the last of it from that S.E. crowd. They'll crow and crow till we get a pain in the ears! No, we can't have that!' he went on, swinging his legs out of bed and reaching for his slacks. 'What are Maclaren and Mahoney doing?'

'They've gone up to the sheds,' grinned Wat Tyler. 'They've gone Hun-mad!'

'I should think they have. I'm not stopping to wash. I'll grab a cup of coffee and a handful of toast as I go through the mess. If you're going up to the office, you might give Flight-Sergeant Smyth a ring. Tell him to get my machine out and start it up.'

'I will,' agreed Tyler, departing.

Two minutes later Biggles burst into the dining-room like a whirlwind, scattering the semi-clad pilots who were calmly preparing for breakfast.

'Come on! Get up into the air, some of you,' he raved, 'or Squadron No. 287 will get every Hun in the sky!'

'Wilks has got another,' said a voice from the window. It was Tyler.

'Another! Who said so?' demanded Biggles.

'I've just got it over the phone!'

'Suffering rattlesnakes!' gasped Biggles. 'This won't do! If he goes on at this rate he'll shoot down the whole blinkin' German air force before we get started! Four, eh? And it's only seven o'clock. He's got the rest of the day in front of him!' he grumbled, as he strode briskly towards the sheds.

Biggles' Camel was out and ticking over on the tarmac when he reached the sheds, and he at once climbed into his seat, and after running the engine to make sure she was giving her full revs, he took off.

He made straight for the Lines, getting as much height as possible as he went. When he got there—to use the old tag—the cupboard was bare. To left and right the sky was empty, except where, far to the north, a trail of fast-diminishing black archie smoke marked the course of a British machine.

Still circling, he pushed further into the blue, as enemy sky was called, searching for something on which to relieve his pent-up anxiety. But in vain.

For an hour he flew up and down, ignoring archie, but the only two machines he saw were a Camel in the distance—probably a machine of his own squadron—and a lonely R.E.8*, far below, spotting for the artillery.

The wind freshened, bringing with it heavy masses of cloud. But it made no difference; not a Hun was to be seen. He spotted a German balloon that had been sent up to take a peep at the British Lines, and he darted towards it. But the watchful crew saw him coming while he was still far away, and by the time he reached the spot the balloon had been hauled down to safety.

Another hour passed, and at the end of it he was fuming with anger and impatience. Two hours, and not a shot had he fired. Fed-up, he turned towards home in order to refuel, for his tanks were nearly empty.

A big cloud lay ahead, and disdaining to go round

* British two-seater biplane designed for reconnaissance and artillery observation.

82

it, he plunged straight through. As he emerged on the opposite side he nearly collided with a big dark green two-seater machine, whose wings were blotched with an unusual honeycomb design.

The type was new to him, but its lines told him at once that it was a German. It was, in fact, a Hannoverana*, a type that had only just made its appearance.

The pilot of the German machine swerved as violently as Biggles did, to avoid collision, and pushing his nose down he streaked for the cloud from which Biggles had so opportunely—or, from the German's point of view, inopportunely—appeared.

In his anxiety that it should not escape, Biggles threw caution to the winds, and without a glance around for possible danger, he roared down and then up under the Hannoverana's tail, raking it with a long burst of bullets as he came.

He saw the machine jerk upwards spasmodically, which told him plainly that the pilot had been hit. The green machine went into a spin, and he watched it suspiciously for a moment. But it was no trick.

The unfortunate observer in the Boche two-seater managed to pull the machine out of the spin near the ground, and did his best to land. But it was not a good effort, and he piled up, a tangled, splintered wreck, in the tree-tops of the Forest of Foucancourt.

Only then did Biggles look up. He saw with a shock that a second machine was alongside him. Fortunately it was a British plane—an S.E.5—but his relief received a check when he realised that it would have been all the same if it had been a Hun.

The pilot of the S.E.5 was gesticulating wildly. But Biggles had no time to wonder what it was all about,

---

* German two-seater fighter and ground attack biplane.

for his tank might run dry at any moment. He put down his nose and raced across the Lines to the aerodrome, which he reached just as his propeller gave a final kick and stopped. He landed with a 'dead stick'; in other words, a silent engine and stationary propeller.

He was beckoning to the mechanics to come and pull the machine in, when he saw to his surprise that the S.E.5 had evidently followed him, for it was landing near the hangars.

Jumping out of the machine, he walked quickly towards the mess, intending to have a cup of coffee while his machine was being refuelled, and it was only when he drew close that he recognised the S.E.5 pilot as Wilkinson.

The other pilot's first words made Biggles pull up in astonishment.

'What's the big idea?' asked Wilks angrily. 'That was my Hun!'

'Your Hun! What are you talking about?' retorted Biggles.

'I'd been stalking that Hun for thirty minutes, and was just in range when you butted in!'

'What's that got to do with me?' Biggles demanded. 'I don't care two flips of a lamb's tail if you've been stalking it for thirty years. I got it, and now I'm going to ask Tyler to get confirmation.'

'I say that I should have had that Hun in another ten seconds!' protested Wilks.

'Then you were just ten seconds too late!' returned Biggles coldly. 'You shouldn't waste so much time.'

'You wouldn't have got him but for me. He was keeping his eye on me, and he didn't even see you. You didn't give him a chance for a shot!'

'By James, you're right!' agreed Biggles. 'I took thundering good care not to. What do you think I am—a target?'

'I say we ought to go fifty-fifty in the claim,' insisted Wilks.

'Fifty-fifty, my foot!' growled Biggles. 'You seem to have the idea that Boche machines are sent up specially for your benefit, so that you can knock them down. Let me tell you that the birds that flit about these pastures are as much mine as yours.

'If you don't like it go and find yourself another playground. Better still, drop a note at Douai and ask the Huns to send some more machines up. I got that one, and I'm not sharing it with anyone. If you choose to spend half an hour trying to get close enough to a Hun for a shot, that's your affair. Cheerio!'

With a wave of his hand Biggles passed on towards the squadron office.

When he returned, twenty minutes later, the S.E. had disappeared, and he grinned at the flight-sergeant who had overheard the conversation.

'I'm afraid that was a bit tough on Captain Wilkinson,' he said. 'But when this game gets so that one has to sit back and let someone else have the first pop, I'm through with it. First come, first served is the motto!'

'That's what I say!' grinned the flight-sergeant.

'You don't know anything about it,' Biggles told him calmly. 'Are my tanks filled?'

'Yes, sir.'

'Right. Then give me a swing.'

As he flew once more in the direction of the battle-field, Biggles derived some comfort from the fact that Wilks had added nothing to his score, a fact that he had ascertained from Tyler, who had been in telephone conversation with No. 287 Squadron office. Several officers of the Camel squadron had been back for more petrol, but not one of them had had a combat. Mahoney, the flight-commander, he learned, was now leading the morning patrol.

On reaching the Lines, Biggles began a repetition of his earlier show, seeking the elusive black-crossed machines. But there wasn't an enemy machine to be seen. He penetrated far into enemy country, but realising that even if he did meet a Hun and bring it down, it would be out of sight of watchers along the Line, he turned his nose towards home.

The ceaseless watching began to tire him, for not for a moment could a single-seater pilot over the Lines afford to allow his eyes to rest. An instant's lack of vigilance might be paid for with his life.

Another two hours passed slowly and he began to edge towards Maranique, for fifteen minutes would see his tanks empty again. He glanced towards the Lines, and suddenly a shadow fell across his machine.

The quick jerk of his head, the spasmodic movements of hand and foot on control-stick and rudder-bar were simultaneous with the clatter of his guns. At his second shot a yellow Albatross, twenty yards above and in front of him, burst into flames.

The whole thing had happened in a split second and was a graphic example of the incredible co-ordination of brain and action that was developed by the expert air fighter. There was no time for thought. The movements, from the moment the shadow had fallen across him, were separate in themselves, yet they had followed each other in such quick succession that they appeared to be only one.

First he had looked to see what had thrown the shadow, then his head had moved forward so that his eye came in line with the gun-sight, he had adjusted his position with stick and rudder, and his hand had gripped the gun lever and pressed it. All that had happened in less than one second of time. He had hit his target, and he knew he would never make a better shot in his life.

He did not actually see the burning machine crash, for as his second shot took effect, he jerked his head round to ascertain if the machine was alone or one of a formation. To his utter astonishment he saw an S.E.5 whirl past him, pull up in a steep climbing turn, half roll on top, and come roaring back.

As he passed, the pilot shook his clenched fist and Biggles recognised Wilks' machine.

'Great Scott, I believe I've done it again!' he muttered, and then laughed as the funny side struck him.

As he raced back to Maranique he tried to work out what had happened. The Albatross must have been diving for home with Wilks in pursuit, in which case it was unlikely that the German pilot had even seen him, as he would naturally be looking back over his shoulder at the pursuing machine. By an unlucky chance for himself the German had chosen a course that took him between Biggles and the sun, with the result that his machine had thrown a shadow on the Camel.

That must have been how it happened, Biggles decided, and he was not surprised to see the S.E.5 land a few yards in front of him. Wilkinson was white with anger.

'All right, keep calm! You're not going to tell me that I pinched your Hun on purpose!' cried Biggles as he approached.

'Did it on purpose! It was an absolute fluke!' snapped Wilks. 'Why, you never even saw him, and he was coming down on you like a sack of bricks.'

'Coming down on me?' Biggles queried.

'That's what I said. He was after you, and he'd got you stone cold. He was up in the sun, and you never even saw him. I spotted him, though, and came down to save your useless hide. He happened to look back and see me, and it put him off his stroke. If I hadn't been there he would have cut you in halves, and you wouldn't have known what had hit you.'

'If that's so, then I can only say that I am very much obliged to you,' observed Biggles casually. 'Don't get the idea that I need a nurse, though.'

'Is that all you have to say?'

'What else do you expect? Do you want me to burst into tears?'

'No; but as we were both in at the death, I don't think you can rightly claim that Hun.'

'Can't I?' exploded Biggles. 'You'll jolly well see whether I can or not! If you go hanging about where I am in order to watch me perform, that's no business of mine. Really, I ought to make a charge for giving you instruction in Hun-getting. No, Wilks, if you've got a grouse, you run away and play by yourself. Have you got any more Huns by the way?'

'No, but I should if you hadn't barged in.'

'Oh, don't let's go over it all again!' protested Biggles.

Wilks glared.

'All right,' he said. 'But you keep out of my way!'

And with that parting shot he strode back to his machine.

Biggles watched him go with quiet amusement, and then turned to see his machine refuelled, after which he went down to the mess for a rest and an early lunch.

# Chapter 10
# Biggles' Bombshell!

Biggles' third victory that day was a straightforward duel which was won fairly and squarely by superb flying and shooting, and only then after one of the longest and most hair-raising combats that had fallen to his experience.

The victim was the pilot of a Fokker Triplane\*, who was cruising about, apparently looking for trouble in the same manner as the Camel pilot. They spotted each other at the same moment, and turned towards one another, so there was no question of pursuit.

The German seemed to be as anxious for the combat as Biggles, and the opening spars were sufficient to warn Biggles that he had caught a tartar. Not that he minded. If a Hun was a better man that he was, then he—Biggles—would have to pay the penalty. That was a maxim that long ago he had laid down, and at first it rather looked as if this might prove to be the very man.

To describe the combat in detail, move and counter-move, would be like cataloguing the moves in a game of chess, and boring accordingly, but it must be mentioned that by the end of a quarter of an hour neither had gained an advantage or given the other a reasonable opportunity for a shot, although a lot of ammunition had been expended.

Biggles' early impetuosity received a check when he

---

\* German fighter with three wings on each side of the fuselage, with two forward-firing guns.

got a burst from the other's gun through his fuselage, one shot razing the back of his helmet. After that he settled himself down to cold, calculating fighting.

The opening stages of the duel took place immediately over the Lines, but as it progressed the two machines drifted with the prevailing wind further and further into enemy territory, and this was the only point that caused Biggles any real concern, for it was a very definite disadvantage. The Triplane could outclimb him, but he could turn faster and dive more steeply, for the Fokker's well-known structural weakness prevented it from diving very fast, except at the risk of losing its wings.

Banking, climbing, and zooming, they fought on, the rest of the world forgotten. Both had opportunities to break away, but both refused to take them, preferring to see the thing through to the end. Several times the machines passed so close that the pilots could see each other's faces.

The German, Biggles saw, was a clean-shaven young fellow of about his own age. He wore goggles but no flying helmet, and his long flaxen hair quivered in the rush of the slipstream.

Biggles' ammunition was running low, and he knew that at any moment it might run right out. Then the end came—suddenly.

Both pilots found themselves facing each other at a distance of not more than a hundred feet. Both started shooting, the tracer bullets making a glittering streak between them.

Biggles knew that collision was inevitable unless the German turned, for he himself had no intention of turning; nor did he expect the other to give way. He had already braced himself for the crash when suddenly the Triplane lunged downwards and passed underneath him.

He was round in a flash, expecting it to come up behind him. But it did not. It was going down in an erratic glide towards the ground with the engine cut off. That the machine was in difficulties was clear, and presently, as he went down behind it, Biggles saw the reason. An elevator hinge of the German plane had been cut clean through, and the elevator itself was wobbling, as though it were likely to fall off at any moment.

Biggles did not use his guns again, although a finishing shot would have been a simple matter. Instead, he watched the pilot make a gallant attempt to land in a field that was much too small, and crash into the hedge on the far side. The unlucky pilot extricated himself quickly, apparently unhurt, and, looking upwards, waved cheerfully to his conqueror.

After an answering wave, Biggles returned once more to Maranique to report the affair in order that confirmation could be obtained by a reconnaissance machine before the Germans had time to remove the crashed plane. And he wanted to have new belts of ammunition put in his guns.

On the tarmac he was greeted by Mahoney, who informed him that Wilks had had no more luck.

'Then he's still one ahead of me,' observed Biggles. 'I shall have to try to even things up!'

'If you can get another, you'll be O.K.; Wilks won't get any more today.'

'How's that?' Biggles asked.

'He took on a Hun over Mossyface Wood, and the gunner nearly got him first burst. A bullet grazed his arm and took the tip off the middle finger of his left hand. The doctor has packed him off to hospital to have his finger dressed. Believe me, Wilks is as sore as a bear!'

'So I should think! I call that tough,' replied Biggles, with real sympathy. 'Smyth,' he went on, turning towards the flight-sergeant, 'get some patches put over these holes, and have a good look round, will you?' He pointed to the bullet holes in his fuselage. 'And have her ready as soon as you can. Ring up the mess and let me know when she's finished.'

'Very good, sir!'

The work of repairing the damaged machine took longer than Biggles expected. Thirty bullets had gone through it, and one had nicked the control-stick, necessitating a replacement.

And so it was well on in the afternoon before Biggles was in the air again, in a final attempt to 'level up' with Wilks, and, if possible, beat him.

It is a curious fact that no two air combats are fought in quite the same way, and Biggles' fourth and final affair of this surprising day was no exception to the rule. It may have been his most unusual conquest; certainly it was the most spectacular from his point of view!

When he took off on this last flight he had already put in six hours' flying that day, which was more than enough for any man. He was desperately tired, but his keenness to add another to his score and thus take the gilt off Squadron No. 287's ginger-bread—as he put it—urged him on.

He scoured the sky in all directions for more than two hours, but not a single hostile aircraft did he see. He didn't know that nearly all the enemy squadrons normally stationed in that sector of the Line had been moved further south in readiness for a big attack that was due to be launched the following morning! All he knew was that the sky, for some reason or other, was completely deserted.

He hung on until it was nearly dark, by which time he had only two or three minutes' supply of petrol left; then he was compelled to return home empty-handed.

92

As a matter of fact, he did not reach Maranique. He finished the patrol far to the north of his usual haunts, and rather than risk a forced landing by running out of petrol he dropped in at the first aerodrome he reached, in order to pick up sufficient fuel to see him home.

But such was the hospitality of the R.F.C. pilots, among whom he found himself, that he stayed on, and finally allowed himself to be persuaded to dine with them.

Having made this decision he went, as a matter of duty, to the telephone, and rang up his own squadron office to let them know that he was safely down.

'You'd better stay where you are for the night,' Tyler told him from the other end of the telephone. 'You'd be crazy to try flying back in the dark. Or, if you like, I'll send a tender* for you. By the way, did you get another Hun?'

'No, worse luck!' replied Biggles ruefully.

'Pity! Wilks has just rung up. He says that he and a whole crowd of them are coming over here from Squadron No. 287 tonight—so we know what to expect!'

'Is he?' observed Biggles, thinking hard. 'Oh, well, it can't be helped! Send a tender over, about ten, will you, Tyler, and I'll come home to bed.'

'I will. Cheerio!'

It was nearly half-past ten that night when Biggles finally reached home. He found the mess choc-a-bloc with officers, for Wilks and his S.E.5 pilots, knowing that he was coming back, had deliberately delayed their departure until he returned.

His entry was heralded by a derisive cheer from the S.E. pilots and yells of protest from the Camel pilots.

* Vehicle generally used for moving supplies.

'What's all the noise about?' asked Biggles, as he threw himself into an easy chair. 'Has somebody in your crowd found a shilling, Wilks, and got all excited about it?'

'No!' Wilks told him. 'We are just feeling a bit on our toes. Don't pretend you don't know why. Tough luck, laddie!'

'What are you tough-lucking me for?' asked Biggles, with well-feigned astonishment.

'Because we've shown you that S.E.'s are the real Hun-getters!' retorted Wilks.

'How do you make that out?'

'I've proved it by getting four Huns to your three—in spite of the fact that two of yours should really have been mine!' claimed Wilks.

'So that's what you're all crowing about!'

'It's enough, isn't it?' Wilks retorted.

'Just because you've got four miserable Huns?' laughed Biggles.

'That's more than you could do, anyway?'

'Where did you get that idea?'

'Tyler admitted it. He told us long after it was dark that you'd rang up to say you'd got no more.'

'Tyler always was a bit behind the times,' Biggles observed, yawning. 'Anyway, that was at half-past eight. At half-past nine I shot down a night-raiding Gotha* over Amiens!

'It's a mistake to count your chickens before they're hatched!' he concluded, amid a mighty roar of laughter from the assembled Camel pilots.

---

* German twin-engined biplane bomber with a crew of three which carried a maximum of fourteen bombs, weighing a total of 1100 lbs.

94

# Chapter 11
# The Camera

Biggles landed, taxied in, and sat for a moment or two in the cockpit of his Camel plane in front of the hangars of No. 266 Squadron. Then he yawned, switched off, and climbed stiffly to the ground.

'Is she flying all right, sir?' asked Smyth, his flight-sergeant, running up.

'She's inclined to be a bit left wing low—nothing very much, but you might have a look at her.'

'Very good, sir,' replied the N.C.O., feeling the slack flying wires disapprovingly. 'She wasn't like this when you took off, sir.'

'Of course she wasn't! You don't suppose I've just been footling about between here and the Lines, do you?'

'No, sir; but you must have chucked her about a bit to get her into this state.'

Biggles yawned again, for he had been flying very high and was tired; but he did not think it worthwhile to describe a little affair he had had with a German Rumpler plane near Lille. 'Perhaps you're right,' he admitted, and strolled slowly towards the officers' mess.

A hum of conversation came from the ante-room as he opened the door.

'What's all the noise about?' he asked, as he sank down into a chair.

'Mac was just talking about narrow escapes,' replied Mahoney.

'Narrow escapes? What are they?' he asked curiously.

95

'Why, don't you have any?' inquired Algy Lacey, who had joined the squadron not long before.

'It depends what you call "narrow",' Biggles replied.

'Oh, hallo, Bigglesworth! There you are!' said the C.O., from the door. 'Come outside a minute, will you? Major Raymond, from Wing Headquarters, wants a word with you,' he went on as the door closed behind them.

Biggles saluted and then shook hands with the Wing officer.

'I've got a job for you, my boy,' smiled the major.

Biggles grinned.

'I was hoping you'd just called to ask how I was,' he murmured.

'I've no time for pleasure trips,' laughed the major. 'But seriously, this is really something in your line, although to be quite fair, I've put the same proposition to two or three other officers whom I can trust, in the hope that someone will succeed if the others fail.'

'Is Wilks—Wilkinson, I mean—one of them?' asked Biggles.

'Yes, and with an S.E.5 he might stand a better chance of success than you do in a Camel.'

Biggles stiffened.

'I see,' he said shortly. 'What is—'

'I'm coming to that now,' broke in the major. 'By the way, what do you think of this?'

He passed an enlarged photograph.

Biggles took it and stared at it with real interest, for it was the most perfect example of air photography he had ever seen. Although it must have been taken from a great height, every road, trench, tree and building stood out as clearly as if it had been taken from a thousand feet or less.

96

'By jingo, that's a smasher!' he muttered. 'Is it one of ours?'

'Yes; but I'm afraid it's the last one we shall ever get like it,' replied the major.

Biggles looked up with a puzzled expression.

'How's that?' he asked quickly.

'The Huns are using that camera now.'

'Camera! Why, is there only one of them?'

'There is only one camera in the world that can take a photograph as perfect as that, and the Germans produced it. It's all in the lens, of course, and I've an idea that that particular lens was never originally intended for a camera.

'It may have been specially ground for a telescope, or microscope, but that is really neither here or there. As far as we are concerned, the Germans adapted it for a camera, and we soon knew about it by the quality of the photographs that fell into our hands from German machines that came down over our side of the Lines.

'I will give you the facts, although I must be brief, as I have much to do. About three months ago we had a stroke of luck—a stroke that we never expected. The machine that was carrying the camera force-landed over our side, although force-landed is hardly the word. Apparently it came down rather low to avoid cloud interference, and the pilot was killed outright by archie, in the air. The observer was wounded, but he managed to get the machine down after a fashion.

'As soon as he was on the ground he fainted, which may account for the fact that he did not destroy or conceal the camera before he was taken prisoner. That was how the camera fell into our hands, and we lost no time in putting it to work. Needless to say, we took every possible precaution to prevent the Germans getting it back again.

'We had it fitted to a special D.H. 4,* the pilot of which had orders on no account to cross the Lines below eighteen thousand feet. Naturally, we had to send the machine over the Lines, otherwise the instrument would have been no use to us; we didn't want photographs of our own positions.

'This pilot also had instructions to avoid combat at all costs, but if he did get into trouble, he was to throw the camera overboard, or do anything he liked with it as long as the Germans didn't get hold of it again.'

'What was to prevent the Huns making another camera like it? Couldn't they make another lens?' asked Biggles.

'Good gracious, no! A lens of that sort takes years and years of grinding to make it perfect. I doubt if that particular one was produced inside five years, and being worked on all the time.'

'I see.'

'Well, you will be sorry to hear that the camera is now in German hands again.'

'How the dickens did they get it?' exclaimed Biggles.

The major made a wry face and shrugged his shoulders.

'We may learn after the war is over,' he said. 'Perhaps we shall never know. The two officers who were in the D.H. 4 are both prisoners, so we have no means of finding out. One can only imagine that they were shot down, or were forced down by structural failure, although how and why they failed to destroy the camera, knowing its vital importance, is a mystery.

'We were sorry when the machine failed to return—

* de Havilland 4 – British two-seater day bomber 1917–1920. W. E. Johns piloted the D.H.4 with 55 Squadron in 1918.

98

and we were astounded when the Germans began using the camera again, because we felt certain that our fellows would have disposed of it, somehow or other. Naturally, if the machine had been shot down from a great height, or in flames, the camera would have been ruined. Well, there it is.

'Our agents in Germany have confirmed the story. They say that the Germans have the camera, and are tickled to death about it. To make sure that they don't lose it again, they've built a special machine to carry it, and that machine is now operating over our Lines at an enormous altitude.'

'What type of machine?' asked Biggles.

'Ah, that we don't know!'

'Then you don't know where it is operating, or what limit of climb it's got?'

'On the contrary,' the major replied, 'we have every reason to believe that it is now operating over this very sector. The archie gunners have reported a machine flying at a colossal height, outside the range of their guns. They estimate the height at twenty-four thousand feet.'

'What!' Biggles exclaimed. 'How am I going to get up there? I can't fly higher than my Camel will go!'

'That is for you to work out. We are having a special machine built, but it will be two or three months before it is ready. Meanwhile, we have got to stop the Germans using that instrument. If we can get it back intact, so much the better. Rather than let the Germans retain it, we would destroy it: but, naturally, we should like to get it back.'

'If the machine was shot down and crashed, or fell in flames, that would be the end of the camera?' Biggles queried. 'And if the crew found they were forced to land, they would throw the thing overboard, in which case it would be busted?'

'Unquestionably.'

Biggles scratched his head.

'You seem to have set a pretty problem,' he observed. 'If we don't shoot the machine down, we don't get the camera. If we do shoot it down, we lose it. That's what it amounts to. Puzzle—how to get the camera! Bit of a conundrum, isn't it?'

'Well, there must be an answer,' smiled the major, 'because it has already been captured twice. We got it once and the Germans got it back.'

'Well, sir, I'm no magician, but I'll do my best.'

'Think it over—and let me know when you've got it.'

Biggles walked back to the ante-room, deep in thought.

'Let him know when I've got it, eh?' he mused. 'By James, what a nerve!'

# Chapter 12
# Thumbs to Noses!

Later in the day a lot of cloud blew up from the south and west, and as this would, he knew, effectually prevent high altitude photography, Biggles did no flying, but roamed about the sheds trying to find a solution to the difficult problem that confronted him. Finally, he went to bed, still unable to see how the impossible could be accomplished.

He was still in bed the following morning—for Mahoney was leading the dawn patrol—when an orderly-room clerk awakened him by rapping on his door and handing in a message.

Biggles took the strip of paper, looked at it, then leapt out of bed as if he had been stung. It was from the Operations Office, Wing Headquarters, and was initialled by Major Raymond.

'High altitude reconnaissance biplane crossed the Lines at seven-twenty-three near Bethune,' he read.

That was all. The message did not state that the machine was the machine, but the suggestion was obvious. So pulling a thick sweater over his pyjamas and hastily climbing into his flying-suit, he made for the sheds without even stopping for the customary cup of tea and a biscuit.

He fumed impatiently in the cockpit of his Camel until the engine was warm enough to take off, and then streaked into the air in the direction of the last known position of the enemy machine.

While still some distance away from Bethune he saw

two S.E.5's climbing fast in the same direction, but paid no further heed to them, for he had also seen a long white line of white archie bursts making a trail across the blue of the early morning sky.

By raising his goggles and riveting his eyes on the head of the trail of smoke, he could just see the tiny sparks of white light from the blazing archie as the gunners followed the raider, who was, however, still invisible.

'By James, he's high, and no mistake!' thought Biggles, as he altered his course slightly, to cut between the hostile machine and the Lines, noticing that the two British S.E.5's carried on the pursuit on a direct course for the objective.

Five minutes later, at fifteen thousand feet, he could just see the Hun, a tiny black speck winging slowly through the blue just in front of the nearest archie bursts. Another ten minutes passed, during which time he added another two thousand feet to his altitude, and he could then see the machine plainly.

'That plane came out of the Halberstadt works, I'll bet my shirt!' he mused, as he watched it closely. 'There is no mistaking the cut. Well, I expect that's it!' he declared, as the terrific height at which the machine was flying became apparent. He had never seen an aeroplane flying so high before, and from the major's description it could only be the special photographic plane.

It did not take him long to realise that any hopes he may have had of engaging it in combat were not to be fulfilled, for although he could manage twenty thousand feet, the enemy plane was still a good two thousand feet above him.

To his intense annoyance, it actually glided down a little way towards him, and he distinctly saw the observer produce a small camera and take a photograph of him.

'That's to show his pals what a lot of poor boobs we are, I suspect!' Biggles muttered, and then a slight flush tinged his cheeks as the observer leaned far out of his cockpit and put his thumb to his nose to express his contempt.

'So that's how you feel, is it, you pudding-faced sausage guzzler?' snarled Biggles. 'That's where you spoil yourself. I'm going to get you, sooner or later, if I have to sprout wings out of my shoulder-blades to do it!'

An S.E.5 sailed across his field of view, nose up and tail dragging at stalling-point as the propeller strove to grasp the thin air. As he watched, the machine slipped off on to one wing and lost a full thousand feet of height before the pilot could recover control.

He recognised the machine as Wilkinson's, from the neighbouring squadron, and could well imagine the pilot's disgust, for it would take him a good twenty minutes to recover his lost height.

'Ugh, it's perishing cold up here!' he muttered, as he wiped the frost from his windscreen, and then turned his attention again to the Hun, who was now flying to and fro methodically in the recognised manner of a photographic plane obtaining strip photographs of a certain area. Looking down, Biggles saw that it was over a large British rest-camp.

'I'd better warn those lads when I get back that they are likely to have a bunch of bombs unloaded on 'em tonight,' he thought, guessing that before the day was out the photographs now being taken by the black-crossed machine would be in the hands of the German bomber squadrons.

'Well, I suppose it's no use sitting up here and getting frost-bitten,' he continued morosely, as he saw the S.E. abandon the chase and begin a long glide back towards its aerodrome. 'Still, I'll just leave you my card.'

He put his nose down to gather all the speed possible, and then, pulling the control-stick back until it touched his safety-belt, he stood the Camel on its tail and sprayed the distant target with his guns. He was still at a range at which shooting was really a waste of ammunition, but he derived a little satisfaction from the action. The Camel hung in the air for a second, with vainly threshing prop, and a line of tracer bullets streaked upwards.

The enemy observer apparently guessed what Biggles was doing, and called the pilot's attention, but he did not bother to return the fire. As one man, pilot and observer raised their thumbs to their noses and extended their fingers.

Biggles' face grew crimson with mortification, but he had no time to dwell on the insult, for the nose of the Camel whipped over as it stalled viciously, and only the safety-belt prevented him from being flung over the centre section. From the stall the machine went into a spin, from which he could not pull it out until he was down at eighteen thousand feet.

For a moment he thought of going over the Lines in search of something on which to vent his anger, but the chilly atmosphere had given him a keen appetite, and he decided to go home for some breakfast instead, and he turned his nose towards Maranique. Looking back, he could still see the enemy pilot pursuing his leisurely way.

After a quick breakfast, he returned to the sheds, and called Smyth, his flight-sergeant, to one side.

'Now,' he began, 'by hook or by crook, I've got to

put three thousand feet on to the limit of climb of this plane!'

The N.C.O. opened his eyes in surprise, then shook his head.

'That's impossible, sir,' he said.

'I knew you'd say that,' replied Biggles, 'but it's only because you haven't stopped to think. Now, suppose some tyrant had you in his power and promised to torture you slowly to the most frightful death if you couldn't put a few more feet on to the altitude performance of a Camel plane, what would you say?'

The flight-sergeant hesitated.

'Well, in that case, sir, I believe—'

'You don't believe!' retorted Biggles. 'You know jolly well you'd do it; you'd employ every trick you knew to stick those extra few feet on. Very well; now let us get down to it and see what we can do. First of all, what weight can we take off her? Every pound we take off means so many feet extra climb—that's right, isn't it?'

'Quite right, sir.'

'Well, then, first of all we can take the tank out and put a smaller one in holding, say, an hour's petrol. Instead of carrying the usual twenty-six gallons, I'll carry ten, which should save about a hundred pounds, for a rough guess. That means I can climb faster from the moment I take off. All the instruments can come out, and I can cut two ammunition-belts to fifty rounds each.

'If I can't hit him with a hundred rounds, he deserves to get away. If you can think of anything else to strip off, take it off. Talking of ammunition reminds me that I want the cut belts filled with ordinary bullets, not tracer bullets—I don't want to set fire to anything. So much for the weight. Now, can you put a few more horses in the engine?'

'I could, but I wouldn't guarantee how long it would last.'

'No matter—do it. If it will last an hour, that's all I want. And you can get some fellows polishing up the struts and fabric—and the prop. Skin friction takes off more miles an hour than a lot of people imagine. Now, is there any way that we can tack on some more lift? It isn't speed I want, it's climb. And do you think we could build extensions on the wing-tips? Every inch of plane-surface helps.'

'If we did,' answered the flight-sergeant, 'the machine would be a death-trap; they'd come off at the slightest strain.'

'Still, it could be done.'

The flight-sergeant thought hard for a moment.

'I'll take the fabric off and look at the main spar,' he said quickly. 'I've got two or three old wings about, so I should have material. I'm afraid the extensions would break away, though, or pull the whole plane clean off. The C.O.—'

'Don't you say a word about this to the C.O. He'd want me to go down to the repair depot, and you know what they'd do—they'd just laugh their silly heads off. Well, you have a shot at it, flight-sergeant—I'll give you until tomorrow morning to finish.'

'Tomorrow morning! It would take two or three days to do, even if it is possible!'

Biggles tapped him on the shoulder.

'I shall be along at sparrow-chirp tomorrow morning, and if that kite isn't ready to fly, and, what is more, fly to twenty-three thousand feet up, someone will get it in the neck!'

'Very good, sir,' replied the flight-sergeant grimly.

He had been set a difficult task—almost an imposs-

ible one; but he knew when Biggles spoke in that tone
of voice it was useless to argue. He got busy right away.
And Biggles walked briskly back to the mess.

107

# Chapter 13
# What a Bullet Did

True to his word, Biggles strode across the dew-soaked turf towards the sheds the following morning as the first grey streak appeared in the eastern sky, having already rung up Wing Headquarters and asked that he might be informed at once if the high-flying German photographic machine was observed to cross the Lines within striking distance of Maranique.

A broad smile spread over his face as his eyes fell on his machine, to which a party of weary mechanics, who had evidently been up all night, were just putting the finishing touches.

Every spot of oil and every speck of dust had been removed from wings and fuselage, while the propeller gleamed like a mirror; but it was not that that made him smile. It was the extensions, for the top planes now overlapped the lower ones by a good eighteen inches.

'It looks pretty ghastly, I must say,' he confessed to the flight-sergeant, who was superintending his handiwork with grim satisfaction. 'Any of our lads who happen to see me in the air are likely to throw a fit.'

Smyth nodded.

'Yes, sir,' was all he said, but it was as well that Biggles did not know what was passing in his mind.

'Well, let's get her out on to the tarmac ready to take off,' ordered Biggles.

'Are you going to test her, sir?'

'I most certainly am not; there's no sense in taking

risks for nothing. I can do all the testing I need when I'm actually on the job.'

After a swift glance around to make sure no one was about, they wheeled the modified Camel out on to the tarmac. A mechanic took his place by the propeller ready to start up, and Biggles donned his flying kit.

The minutes passed slowly as the sky grew gradually lighter, and Biggles began to fear that the enemy machine was not going to put in an appearance. Just as he had given up hope, Wat Tyler, the recording officer, appeared, running, with a strip of paper in his hand. He stopped dead and recoiled as his eyes fell on the Camel's wing-tips, conspicuous in their incongruity.

'What the—what the—' he gasped.

'She's all right—don't worry,' Biggles told him. 'Her wings have sprouted a bit in the night, that's all. Is that message for me?'

'Yes. The German machine crossed the Lines about four minutes ago, between Bethune and Annoeulin, following the Bethune-Treizennes road. Wing have discovered that it is attached to the Fleiger Abteilung at Seclin.'

'Thanks!' replied Biggles, and climbed into his seat. He waved the chocks away after the engine had been run up, and taxied slowly out into position to take-off. 'Well, here goes!' he muttered, as he opened the throttle.

The lightness of the loading was instantly apparent, for the machine came off the ground like a feather—so easily that he was off the ground before he was aware of it.

For some minutes he watched his new wing-tips anxiously, but except for a little vibration they seemed to be functioning perfectly, although a dive would no doubt take them off—and perhaps the wings as well.

Grinning with satisfaction he made for the course of the photograph plane, and, as he had done the previous morning, first picked it out by the line of archie smoke that was expending itself uselessly far below it.

A D.H. 4 that was presumably under test came up and looked at him as he passed over the aerodrome of Chocques, the pilot shaking his head as if he could not believe his eyes.

'He thinks he's seeing things!' smiled Biggles. 'He's going home now to tell the boys about it.' Three S.E.'s were converging on his course some distance ahead, and they all banked sharply to get a clearer view of the apparition. Biggles waved them away, for he had no wish to be compelled to make a steep turn that might spell disaster.

He reached nineteen thousand feet in effortless style, and from the way the machine was behaving he felt that it would make the three or four thousand feet necessary to reach the enemy machine without difficulty.

Progress became slower as he climbed, and the German began to draw away from him, for it was flying level, so he edged his way between it and the Lines and watched for it to make the first move on its return journey.

A joyful song broke from his lips as the Camel climbed higher and higher, for whether he managed to bag the Hun or not he was at least getting a new thrill for his trouble! But soon afterwards he began to feel the effects of the rarefied air, which he had forgotten to take into consideration, so he stopped singing and concentrated his attention on the enemy aircraft, which was, he guessed, probably equipped with oxygen apparatus.

What his own exact altitude was he did not know, for the altimeter had been removed with the other instruments, but he felt that it must be between twenty-two and twenty-three thousand feet. He was still slightly below the Hun, but he felt that he could close the distance when he wished. The other was now flying up and down in regular lines as it had done before, with both members of the crew seemingly intent on their work.

Once, the observer stood up to glance below at where the three British S.E.'s were still circling, and then resumed his task without once glancing in Biggles' direction, and obviously considering himself quite safe from attack.

Slowly but surely Biggles crept up under the enemy's tail, a quiver of excitement running through him as the moment for action drew near.

To force the German machine to land without causing any damage to the camera was a problem for which he had still found no solution unless it was possible for him to hit its propeller, although he had some doubt as to his ability to do that.

He was now within a hundred yards, and still neither of the Germans had seen him. He was tempted to shoot at once, for the machine presented a fairly easy target, but, following his plan of trying to hit the propeller, he put his nose down in order to overtake the big machine and attack it from the front.

Unfortunately, at that moment the German pilot, who had reached the end of his beat, turned; the observer spotted him and jumped for his gun, but he was just too late.

Biggles was already turning to bring his sights to bear; his hand found and pressed the gun lever. Rat-tat-tat-tat!

Biggles may have been lucky, for the result was instantaneous. Splinters flew off the big machine, and it plunged earthwards. As it passed below him Biggles saw the pilot hanging limply forward on his safety-belt, and the observer frantically trying to recover control.

Biggles throttled back and followed it down, and as it came out into a glide he half expected to see the observer make a last attempt to reach the Lines, but either his courage failed him or he was too occupied in controlling the machine, for he made no such attempt.

Biggles waved his arm furiously as the waiting S.E.'s closed in, but they stood aside as victor and vanquished sped through them, with Biggles so close that he could see the German observer's white face.

At a thousand feet from the ground Biggles saw him bend forward and struggle with something on the floor of the cockpit, and guessed that he was endeavouring to release the camera, about which he had no doubt had special instructions.

But the warning rattle of Biggles' guns made him spring up again. In his anxiety he tried to land in a field that was really much too small for such a big machine, with the inevitable result, and it crashed into the trees on the far side.

Biggles was also feeling anxious, for he knew that as soon as he was on the ground the German's first action would be to destroy or hide the camera, so he took a risk that in the ordinary way he would have avoided. He put the machine into a steep side slip and tried to get into the same field.

As he flattened out he knew he had made a mistake, for the machine did not drop as it would normally have

112

done, but continued to glide over the surface of the ground without losing height. The modifications that had been so advantageous a few minutes before were now his undoing, and although he fish-tailed* hard to lose height, he could not get his wheels on to the turf.

At a speed at which the machine would normally have stalled, he was still gliding smoothly two feet above the ground, straight towards his victim. There was no question of turning, and to have forced the machine down would have meant a nasty somersault.

Seeing that a crash was inevitable, Biggles switched off and covered his face with his left arm, and in that position piled his Camel on to the wreckage of its victim.

He disengaged himself with the alacrity of long experience, and leapt clear—for the horror of fire is never far from an airman's mind—and looking round for the observer, he saw him standing a short distance away as if undecided whether to make a bolt for it or submit to capture.

Biggles shouted to him to return, and without waiting to see if he obeyed, set to work to liberate the unfortunate German pilot, who was groaning in his seat.

Biggles derived some satisfaction from the knowledge that he was still alive, and with the assistance of the German observer who came running up when he saw what was happening, they succeeded in getting him clear.

Wilkinson and another pilot came running down the hedge, having landed in the nearest suitable field when they saw the Camel crash.

* A quick side to side movement of the rudder used when landing to slow the machine down by creating extra wind resistance.

'I thought you'd done it that time!' panted Wilkinson, as he came up.

'So did I!' admitted Biggles. 'But I've bust my beautiful aeroplane; I'm afraid I shall never get another one like it.'

'What— Hallo, here comes Major Raymond,' said Wilkinson. 'He must have been watching the show from the ground; and here's the ambulance coming down the road. The sooner that German pilot is in hospital the better; he's got a nasty one through the shoulder.'

'Is the camera there?' cried Major Raymond, as he ran up, accompanied by two staff officers.

'Camera, sir? By Jove, I'd forgotten it!' replied Biggles. And it was true; in the excitement of the last few minutes all thoughts of the special object of his mission had been forgotten.

'Yes, here it is,' almost shouted the major, tugging at something amongst the debris, regardless of the oil that splashed over his clean whipcord breeches. 'That's lucky—'

He stopped abruptly as several pieces of thick glass fell out of the wide muzzle of the instrument and tinkled amongst the splintered struts. He turned the heavy camera over and pointed accusingly at a round bullet-hole in the metal case, just opposite the lens.

'You've put a bullet right through it!' he cried.

Biggles stared at the hole as if fascinated.

'Well, now, would you believe that?' he muttered disgustedly. 'And they took five years to make it!'

# Chapter 14
# Suspicions

Biggles turned the nose of his Camel plane towards the ghastly ruins of Ypres, still being pounded by bursting shells. He took a final glance at that pulverised strip of Belgium, over which tiny puffs of shrapnel were appearing and fading continuously, then floated away towards the western side of No Man's Land.

His patrol was not yet over, but the deep, pulsating drone of his engine had lost its rhythm as it misfired on one cylinder, and Captain Bigglesworth (his promotion dated from his meritorious work in bringing down the camera-plane) had no desire to become involved in a fight whilst thus handicapped.

Several machines were in the sky, mostly British bombers, for the great battle for possession of the Ypres Salient* was still in progress. But they did not interest him, and he was about to turn his back on the scene when a tiny speck, moving swiftly through the blue, caught his eye.

'That's a Camel! I wonder if it's one of our crowd?' he ruminated as he watched it. 'By James! He's in a hurry, whoever it is!'

The pilot of the approaching Camel was certainly losing no time. With nose well down and tail cocked

---

* A much fought over section of the front line which bulged, sometimes by up to five miles, into German-held territory. It was to the east of the town of Ypres. Over three quarters of a million men on both sides died struggling over possession of this piece of land.

high, the machine sped through the air like a bullet, straight towards the other Camel.

As it drew near, Biggles saw that it was not one of his own squadron—No. 266—nor did he recognise the device, which took the form of two white bands, just aft of the ring-markings on the fuselage.

'There must be a new squadron over,' he thought, as he headed for Maranique, headquarters of his own squadron, noting with surprise that the new arrival changed its course to follow him. It drew still nearer, and finally flew up alongside, the pilot waving a cheerful greeting.

Biggles raised his hand in reply, and a slow smile crept over his face as he examined his companion's machine more closely. At least a dozen neat round holes had been punched in an irregular pattern on the metal engine cowling; there was another straggling group just behind the pilot's seat, and at least twenty more through the tail.

'Gosh, no wonder he was in a hurry!' Biggles muttered.

Presently the aerodrome loomed up ahead and he glided down towards it and slipped in between the hangars. The other machine landed beside him, and side by side they taxied up to the sheds. Biggles pushed up his goggles, threw a leg over the 'hump' of his Camel, slid lightly to the ground, and walked over to the other machine, from which the pilot was just alighting.

"Morning!' he said cheerfully. 'Pity you didn't make a better job of it!'

The stranger looked at him, frowning.

'How so?' he asked.

'I mean, if you could have got a few more holes

116

through your cowling it would have made a sieve; as it is, it's neither one thing nor the other.'

'Never mind, I'll give it to the cook for a colander,' replied the other, smiling. He removed his flying helmet carefully, and looked ruefully at a jagged rent in the ear-flap.

Biggles whistled.

'My word, if that one had been any closer it would have given you a nasty headache!' he exclaimed.

'It would have given my old mother a heartache!' answered the stranger, feeling the side of his head gingerly, where a red weal, just below the ear, told its own story.

'Well, come across to the mess,' invited Biggles. 'By the way, my name's Bigglesworth, of Squadron 266.'

'Mine's Butterworth, of 298.'

'Where do you hang out?' asked Biggles. 'I can't remember seeing any of your fellows in these parts!'

'No,' was the reply. 'We're up on the coast, at Teteghen, doing special escort duty with the day bombers who are operating against the seaplane shed at Ostend. We haven't been over very long.'

'Ostend! Then how did you get right down here?' Biggles wanted to know.

'Just plain curiosity, I guess. I'm not on a "show" today, as a matter of fact, I went up to do a test, and while I was up I thought I'd like to have a look at the Lines. We do most of our flying over the sea, just off the coast, y'know!'

Biggles was still surveying the holes in the machine with a professional eye.

'Quite,' he said slowly. 'But how did you get in this mess?'

Butterworth laughed.

'Serves me right, I suppose,' he said. 'I haven't got

117

a Hun yet, so I thought I'd try to get one. I found one, as you can see—and that's what he did to me!'

'Not too good,' commented Biggles. 'You'll have to fly with Squadron 266 for a bit and learn how to do it. But come along; I expect you can do with some lunch.'

'Sure! I can do with a bite!'

'You're a Canadian, aren't you?' went on Biggles, as they walked in the direction of the officers' mess.

'Yes. What made you think that?'

Biggles laughed.

'People who say "sure" and "I guess" are usually Canadians or Americans, and as you aren't in American uniform—well— Hallo, here comes young Algy Lacey! He's a good scout. You'll like him. What cheer, laddie!' he went on as they met. 'This is Butterworth, of Squadron 298.'

Algy nodded.

'Glad to know you!' he said. 'How did you get on, Biggles?'

'Nothing doing. I didn't see a Hun, and had to pack up after an hour, with a missing engine. Butterworth here kept all the Huns to himself; his kite's got as many holes in it as a petrol-filter. What happened, Butterworth?'

On the mess veranda Butterworth told his story:

'After I left the aerodrome this morning I headed due east for a time, following the Line between Bixshoote and Langemarck. I didn't see a soul, which got a bit boring, so when I got to Wieltje I turned off a bit to the left to see if those German Fokkers and Albatrosses are as common as you fellows pretend.

'For some time I didn't see anyone, except one or two British R.E.8's doing artillery observation duty, and then I suddenly saw five or six Albatrosses on the right of me. I was only about a mile over the Lines—

which didn't seem far from home—but I guess the Huns spotted me just as I spotted them, and as I turned they turned.

'I shan't forget the next five minutes in a hurry. At first I put my nose down and streaked straight down the Lines, trying to out-distance them rather than face them. In other words, I ran away, and I don't mind admitting it. You fellows might think it's good fun taking on half a dozen Huns at once. But not yours truly. I know my limitations.

'The Huns kept pace with me, heading me off from the Line all the time, and then I saw some more Huns coming up from the south. That did it. I got the wind up properly, and just made a wild rush for home; I went right through the middle of the Hun formation, and I reckon I should have bumped into someone if they hadn't got out of my way!

'I clamped on to my gun lever and sprayed the sky. How I got through I don't know, because I could hear their lead boring through my kite several times.

'Well, I got through, as you can see, but it was sheer luck, I guess. I didn't stop till I saw you in the distance; you may have noticed that I made for you like a long-lost brother.'

'What do you suppose you're flying a kite for?' It was Mahoney who spoke; he had approached unobserved. 'To shoot Huns, I suppose,' was the answer.

'You won't get many if you go on like you did this morning!' was Mahoney's retort.

'Oh, give him a chance!' broke in Biggles. 'He hasn't been over here long. D'you really want to get a Hun?' he went on, turning to Butterworth.

'I should say I do!'

'Then suppose we go over together this afternoon and have a look round—that is, you, Algy and me? My engine will be all right by then, and yours only needs a few patches.'

'That's fine! But don't let me butt—'

'Oh, it's a pleasure! We always try to do the best we can for guests. Don't we, Algy?'

'Certainly!'

'That's fine!' declared Butterworth. 'Have a cigarette?' He took a cigarette case from his pocket and offered it. Biggles took it, removed a cigarette, and examined the case with interest. It was a flat one, slightly bent to fit the pocket. Heavily engraved across the corner were the initials F. T. B.

'Nice case,' Biggles observed, handing it back to its owner.

Then Biggles glanced at his watch.

'I think I'll just slip into the office and ring up the sheds to tell them to push on with those machines,' he said. 'Then we had better go in to lunch. Suppose we leave the ground at three?'

'Suits me,' agreed the visitor.

After lunch they reassembled on the veranda for coffee. Biggles drank his quickly, stood the cup and saucer on the window-sill, and looked across to where Butterworth was in conversation with Mahoney and Maclaren.

'I'm just going to slip up to the sheds to see how things are going on,' he said. 'I shan't be more than a couple of minutes. Algy, you'd better come with me to make sure your machine is O.K.'

He picked up his cap and set off towards the hangars, Algy following. On the way, at a point where the hedge met the footpath, he stooped to break off a thin ash stick, which he trimmed of its leaves and twigs as he walked along.

'Are you riding a horse this afternoon?' asked Algy,

as he regarded this unusual procedure with mild interest.

Biggles shook his head.

'At present I'm just riding a hunch—an idea,' he replied mysteriously. 'Wait a minute, and I'll show you.'

Reaching the sheds, Biggles went straight to the visiting Camel. A new cowling* had been fitted, and the riggers were about to patch the holes in the fuselage.

'All right, you can break off for a minute or two,' he told the mechanics. And then, to Algy: 'I want you to take a good look at those holes, to see if you can see anything peculiar about them!'

Algy looked at him in amazement, but examined the holes carefully.

'No, I'm dashed if I can see anything unusual about them,' he admitted, after he had finished his scrutiny. 'They look like good, honest bullet-holes to me!'

'Do you remember me asking Butterworth, at lunch, if he had been under fire before this morning? I asked him the direct question.'

'Yes, I remember perfectly, and he said "No".'

'Then what do you make of this?' Biggles inserted the ash stick in a hole on one side of the fuselage, and pushed it until the point rested in the corresponding hole on the opposite side, where the bullet had emerged.

'I still don't see—' began Algy. But Biggles cut him short.

'Can you tell me how a bullet could pass along a path now indicated by that stick without touching the pilot? It would go through the top part of his leg,

---

* Cover surrounding the engine.

121

wouldn't it? It couldn't possibly miss him entirely, could it?'

'No, it certainly could not!' exclaimed Algy.

'Did you notice Butterworth limping or bleeding, or mentioning being hit? You didn't! Well, I'm as certain as I stand here that Butterworth wasn't in the cockpit of that aeroplane when that bullet was fired!'

'What on earth made you spot that?' gasped Algy.

'You needn't flatter me on account of my eyesight. It was as plain as a pikestaff. At first I simply thought that Butterworth was piling on the agony. There are fellows, you know, who walk about talking as if they were Bishops or McCuddens*, and it adds colour to the tale if there are a few holes in the machine. But let us pass on. This fellow says his name is Butterworth.'

'There's nothing funny about that, is there?'

'There might not be if I didn't happen to know Butterworth personally!' retorted Biggles. 'I met him at Lympne the last time I was in England!'

'There might be two Butterworths!' retorted Algy.

'There might. But it would be a thundering funny coincidence if they both had the same initials—F. T. B.—and the same identical cigarette-case, with the initials engraved in the same way in the same place!'

Algy stared.

'The same cigarette-case?' he gasped.

'That's what I said. Nobody's going to make me believe that there are two such cigarette-cases in the world, both belonging to Butterworths who happen to have the same initials! There is a limit to my imagin-

* William Avery Bishop VC 1894–1956 Canadian fighter pilot with 72 confirmed victories. The 2nd highest scoring RFC pilot in the First World War, M. Mannock VC being the highest with 73 victories. James McCuddens VC 1895–1918 British fighter pilot with 57 confirmed victories (4th highest scorer). Killed in a flying accident in July 1918.

ation. No! Today was not the first time I have taken a cigarette out of the selfsame case that that fellow is now flaunting!

'And I'll tell you why he is flashing it. He put that case on the table to prove, by suggestion, in case there should be any doubt, that his name is Butterworth. Frank Butterworth had that case at Lympne; I've played bridge with him, with the case lying on the table. It was a present from his father, he told me.'

Algy continued to stare.

'Have you finished giving me shocks? I mean, have you any more cards up your sleeve?' he asked.

'Yes, I have; only one, but it's a bone-shaker. Just turn this over in your mind, and see if it suggests anything to you. Frank Butterworth is stationed at Teteghen—or I should say was. He went out on patrol yesterday morning—and went west. He was seen to go down over the German side of the Line, and land.'

'How on earth do you know that?' Algy demanded.

'Because I made it my business to ring up the squadron and find out; that's where I went when I disappeared just before lunch.'

'Then what do you think—now?'

'I'll tell you. I think that Frank Butterworth is either in a German prison hospital, or he's staring up at the sky through four feet of Flanders mud. What is this fellow doing with his cigarette-case? He has got it as a proof of his identity, and I wouldn't mind betting that he has got letters addressed to Butterworth in his pocket!

'What is he doing here—miles away from Teteghen, where Butterworth wouldn't be known? It was a hundred to one against anyone down here knowing Frank Butterworth, but the odd chance has come off.

123

What's his game eh? Work it out for yourself. I'll give you two guesses!'

'Do you think he's a spy?' said Algy thoughtfully.

'What else can I think? I don't want to appear to have a spy complex, but—well, that's what it looks like to me! I should say the fellow is a German-American. There are hundreds of them in America who speak English as well as we do. On the other hand, there is just a chance that he is a British agent up to some game!'

'Can't you ring up someone and find out?'

'I might ring up Raymond, at Wing Headquarters—and be told to mind my own business! In any case, the fellow will have gone before our people do anything. We can't detain him on suspicion!'

'Then what are you going to do about it?'

'I'm going to plant a trap,' said Biggles. 'If he's what he says he is he will come on this trip with me this afternoon; if he isn't, then he won't—at least, I can't imagine him shooting down a Hun machine if he's a Hun himself!

'What is he doing here, at Maranique? Obviously, he is here to pick up all the information he can. Having got it, he'll try to get back to where he came from. On the table in the map-room I've put a map; it shows the aerodromes of as many squadrons as I can think of—but they are not in the right places.

'I want you to go back to the mess and suggest to Butterworth that it might be a good thing if he walked along to the map-room and ascertained the exact position of Maranique, in case he loses us this afternoon. Show him the room, and then leave him there.

'He'll see the map, and I imagine he will try to get away with it, because it would look like a first-class prize to take to Germany.

'If he does pocket it, his next idea will be to get away as soon as he can. By the way, you can tell him that his machine is now O.K.; mention it casually when you leave him in the map-room. If he's on the level, he'll go back to the mess; if he isn't, he'll go up to the sheds and take off.'

'But what about you?' Algy asked. 'He'll be certain to wonder where you are, and what you are doing. What shall I tell him?'

'Tell him I've had an urgent call from an archie battery, and I may be late back. Suggest to him that our proposed trip might have to be postponed for a little while. As a matter of fact, I shall be in the air, high up, watching the aerodrome.

'You will watch him, and if he makes a break for it, run out and wave a towel in front of your room, or wherever you happen to be. That will tell me that he has left the ground. He will probably be surprised to find me upstairs. I shall suggest to him by certain methods that I want him to come back with me. If he doesn't—' Biggles shrugged his shoulders expressively.

'That's my idea, and we'll put it into action right away. Are you sure you've got it quite clear?'

'Absolutely.'

'Good! Then I'll get off!'

# Chapter 15
# Off and Away!

Algy watched Biggles climb into his machine and take off, and then turned and walked thoughtfully towards the mess. Butterworth was still in conversation with Mahoney and several other officers of the squadron who were not on duty.

The man seemed so absolutely at home, so self-possessed and natural in his speech and movements, that a sudden doubt assailed Algy. Suppose Biggles had made a mistake? Spy scares were common in every branch of the fighting services, he knew. That spies operated anywhere and everywhere could not be denied, and some of them with amazing effrontery.

Algy watched the suspected officer closely for some sign or slip that might betray him; but he watched in vain.

'Well, there's no point in wasting time,' he decided, and touched Butterworth on the arm.

'Oh, Butterworth,' he said, 'I've a message for you from Bigglesworth. He's been sent off on a job—had to go and see an archie battery about something—and he may be late back; so this proposed show of ours may have to wait for a little while.

'He will probably be back not later than half-past three; but, in the meantime, he suggests that you have a look round the map-room, so that if you get separated from us during the show you'll know your way back—either here or to your own aerodrome.'

'I see,' replied the other. 'That's not a bad idea! I think I'll follow his advice!'

He picked up his flying-coat, cap and goggles, and threw them carelessly over his arm.

Algy raised his eyebrows.

'You won't want those, will you?' he said.

'I may as well take 'em along; I should only have to come back for them afterwards,' replied Butterworth coolly. 'I don't think too much of the weather,' he went on, looking under his hand towards the horizon, where a dark indigo belt was swiftly rising.

'That looks to me like thunder coming up. If it starts coming across this way, I may push along home without waiting for Bigglesworth to come back. I don't want to get hung up here for the night, and we can postpone the show until another day if necessary!'

Algy's heart missed a beat, for it began to look as if Biggles was right.

'Right-ho!' he said. 'You do just as you like. I'll show you the map-room!'

Together they walked across to the deal and corrugated iron building.

'Here we are!' he said, glancing at the map that had been purposely left lying on the table. 'I think I'll go back to the mess, if you don't mind. Let me know if I can help you.'

'Right-ho! Thanks!'

'And, by the way, you might like to know that your machine is O.K. now.'

'That's fine!'

Algy left the room, closing the door behind him, and passed the window as if he was returning to the mess. But as soon as he was out of sight he doubled back to the rear of the building and quietly placed his eye to a small hole where a knot had fallen out of a board.

Butterworth was bending over the map on the table, studying it carefully. He made a note or calculation on the margin, folded the map, and then walked across to the window. For a moment or two he looked at the sky thoughtfully, and then, as if suddenly making up his mind, he put the map in his pocket, picked up his flying kit, and left the room.

From his place of concealment, Algy watched him walk straight up to the sheds and climb into his machine; a mechanic ran to the propeller, as if Butterworth had called him in a hurry. The engine started, and the machine began to taxi slowly into position for a take-off.

Algy waited for no more. He rushed into the lavatory, tore a towel from its peg, then darted back into the open, waving it above his head. High up in the sky he could just make out Biggles' Camel, circling slowly as it awaited the signal.

'By Jingo, he was right!!' he muttered, as Butterworth's machine took off and headed towards the Line, and the topmost Camel swung round to follow it.

'Is that Butterworth taking off?' said a voice at his elbow.

Algy spun round on his heel, and saw that it was Mahoney who had spoken.

'Yes,' he said quickly.

'Bad show about his brother.'

'Whose brother?' Algy asked.

'Butterworth's brother, of course.'

Algy puckered his forehead.

'Butterworth's brother?' he repeated foolishly.

'What's the matter with you? Have you gone ga-ga or something? I said it was a bad show about his brother being shot down yesterday. He told me about it while you and Biggles were up at the sheds.'

Algy staggered.

'What did he tell you?' he gasped.

'He said that his brother, Frank Butterworth, went West yesterday. They were both in the same squadron. That's his brother's cigarette-case he's got; he borrowed it from him a day or two ago. That's how he came to tell me about it.

'The funny thing was he would have been with his brother but for the fact that he had lent his machine to another fellow just before the show and the fellow went and got himself shot up—got a bullet through the leg. He hasn't even had the Camel patched—Hi! What's wrong with you?'

But Algy wasn't listening. Understanding of the whole situation flooded his brain like a spotlight, and he ran like a madman towards the hangars, praying that he might be in time to prevent a tragedy.

Biggles, sitting in the cramped cockpit of his Camel, eight thousand feet above the aerodrome, stiffened suddenly as he saw Algy's tell-tale signal below, a tiny white spot against the brown earth, and his jaw set grimly as his probing eyes picked out a Camel streaking over the aerodrome at the head of a long trail of dust.

'So Butterworth's making a bolt for it, is he?' he mused. 'Very well, he's got a shock coming to him!'

He swung round, following the same course as the lower Camel, which was apparently climbing very slowly, although it was heading towards the Lines. The thought suddenly struck him that perhaps Butterworth did not intend to climb—that he might streak straight across No Man's Land to the German Lines.

A haze was forming under the atmospheric pressure of the advancing storm, and already the lower machine was no more than a blurred grey shadow. If Biggles didn't hurry he might lose him, after all. He pressed his knees against the side of the cockpit, and eased the control stick forward, gently at first, but with increasing force.

His nose went down, and the quivering needle of the air-speed indicator swung slowly across the dial— 100—120—130—140—The wind howled through the straining wires, and plucked at the top of his helmet with hurricane force.

The low drone of his engine became a shrill wail as the whirling propeller bit the air; the ground floated upwards as if impelled by a hidden mechanism.

At three thousand feet Biggles flattened out, about five hundred feet above and behind the other machine. It was still heading towards the Lines, now not more than a couple of miles away.

Biggles could see Butterworth's helmet clearly; he appeared to be looking at the ground, first over one side of his machine and then the other. Not once did he look about or behind, and Biggles smiled grimly.

'If I was a Hun, you'd be a dead man by now!' he muttered. 'You haven't long to live, if that's your idea of war flying!' It occurred to him that possibly the machine was known to German pilots, who had received instructions not to molest it, but after a moment's reflection he scouted the idea. A German pilot could hardly be expected to examine every Camel he encountered for special marks or signs before he attacked.

He pushed the control-stick forward again, and sped down after his quarry, intending to head him off and signal to him to return. If he refused—well—Biggles' fingers closed over the control of his guns.

At that moment Butterworth looked back over his shoulder.

For one fleeting instant Biggles stared into the goggled face, and then moved like lightning, for the Camel had spun round on its axis, its nose tilted upwards, and a double stream of tracer bullets poured from its guns, making a glittering streak past Biggles' wing-tip.

Biggles kicked out his right foot and flung the control-stick over in a frantic side-slip; for although the attack was utterly unexpected, he did not lose his head, and he was too experienced to take his eyes off his opponent even for a moment. Quick as thought he brought the machine back on to its course, and took the other Camel in his sights.

At that moment Butterworth was within an ace of death. But Biggles did not fire. As his hand squeezed the gun lever for the fatal burst, his head jerked up as something flashed across his sights, between him and his target—a green, shark-like body, from which poured a long streamer of orange flame—a blazing Albatross.

For the next three seconds events moved far more swiftly than they can be described; they moved just as swiftly as Biggles' brain could act and adjust itself to a new set of conditions—conditions that completely revolutionised his preconceived ideas.

After the first shock of seeing the blazing Albatross—for there was no mistaking the German machine—he looked up in the direction whence it had come, and saw five more machines of the same type pouring down in a ragged formation.

He realised instantly that Butterworth had not fired at him, as he had at first supposed, but at the leader of the German planes, and had got him with a piece of brilliant shooting at the first burst.

Butterworth had shot down a Hun!

It meant that something was wrong somewhere, but

there was no time to work it out now. Where was Butterworth? Ah, there he was—actually in front of him, nose tilted upwards, taking the diving Huns head-on!

Biggles roared up to him, peering through his centre section, and his lips parted in a smile as he saw something else. Roaring down behind the rearmost Albatross, at a speed that threatened to take its wings off, was another Camel.

For perhaps three seconds the machines held their relative positions—the two lower Camels side by side, facing the five diving Huns, and the other Camel dropping like a stone behind them.

Then, in a flash, the whole thing collapsed into a whirling dog-fight,* as the Albatrosses pulled out of their dive; that is, all except the last one, which continued its dive straight into the ground. Four against three!

It is almost impossible to recall the actual moves made in an aerial dog-fight; the whole thing afterwards resolves itself into a series of disjointed impressions. Biggles took a dark green machine in his sights, fired, and swerved as he heard bullets hitting his own machine.

He felt, rather than saw, the wheels of another machine whiz past his head, but whether friend or foe he did not know. An Albatross, with a Camel apparently tied to its tail by an invisible cord, tore across his nose; another Camel was going down in a steep side-slip, with a cloud of white vapour streaming from its engine.

Another Albatross floated into his sights; he fired again, and saw it jerk upwards to a whip-stall. He

* An aerial battle rather than a hit-and-run attack.

132

snatched a swift glance over his shoulder for danger, but the sky was empty. He looked around. The air was clear. Turning, he was just in time to see two straight-winged aeroplanes vanishing into the haze.

Below, two ghastly bonfires, towards which people were running, poured dense clouds of black smoke into the air. Near them was a Camel, cocked up on to its nose; some troops were helping the pilot from his seat. Another Camel was climbing up towards him, so he went down to meet it, and saw, as he had already half suspected, that it was Algy's machine.

So it was Butterworth on the ground. What the dickens was he doing, fighting Huns?

There was something wrong somewhere, and the sooner he—Biggles—got back to the aerodrome and found out all about it the better it would be!

Algy was waving, signalling frantically, obviously trying to tell him something. Biggles waved back impatiently, and signalled that he was returning to the aerodrome, where he landed a few minutes later and ran down to the squadron office.

'Have you had any phone messages?' he asked the recording officer.

'Was that you in the mix-up behind Vricourt?' the recording officer wanted to know.

'Yes, me and Algy and Butterworth—you know, the fellow who dropped in to lunch. He's down. Is he hurt?'

'No. Shaken a bit, that's all.'

'Has he gone to hospital?'

'No; he's on his way back here in a tender.'

Biggles went outside and met Algy who had just clambered out of his machine.

Algy looked worried.

'Is he all right?' he called.

133

'If you mean Butterworth—yes.'

'Thank goodness! My word, Biggles, you nearly boobed that time!'

'So it seems. But what do you know about it?'

'It's Butterworth's brother. I mean this fellow is the brother of the fellow you know.'

'Brother?' gasped Biggles.

'Yes. I'll tell you all about it—'

'Shut up—here he comes! Don't, for goodness' sake, say anything about this spy business!'

Butterworth climbed out of the tender that had pulled up on the road, and hurried towards them.

'Say, I guess I've got to thank you for helping me to get that Hun!' Butterworth cried.

'Don't thank me,' replied Biggles—'thank your lucky star. By the way, what made you push off the way you did, without waiting for me to come back?'

Butterworth jerked his thumb upwards towards the darkening sky.

'I thought I'd better try to get home before the storm broke.'

'You pinched the map out of the map-room,' Algy accused him.

'Yes, I know I did,' replied Butterworth. 'I thought I'd take it to make sure of finding my way home. I would have brought it back in a day or two—it would have been an excuse to come. I like you fellows.

'By the way, did I hear you say something to Algy about a spy? I thought I just caught the word.'

'Yes,' replied Biggles. 'But it was only a rumour!'

# Chapter 16
# Turkey Hunting

Biggles stood by the ante-room window of the officers' mess with a coffee cup in his hand and regarded the ever-threatening sky disconsolately.

It was Christmas-time, and winter had long since displaced with its fogs and rains the white, piled clouds of summer, and perfect flying weather was now merely a memory of the past. Nor did the change of season oblige by providing anything more attractive or seasonable than dismal conditions. A good fall of snow would have brightened up both the landscape and the spirits of those who thought that snow and Yuletide ought always to go together; but the outlook from the officers' mess of No. 266 Squadron was the very opposite of what the designers of Christmas cards imagine as an appropriate setting for the season.

'Well,' observed Biggles, as he looked at it, 'I think this is a pretty rotten war! Everything's rotten! The weather's rotten. This coffee's rotten—to say nothing of it being half-cold. That record that Mahoney keeps playing on the gramophone is rotten. And our half-baked mess caterer is rotten—putrid, in fact!'

'Why, what's the matter with him?' asked Wat Tyler, the recording officer, from the table, helping himself to more bacon.

'Tomorrow is Christmas Day, and he tells me he hasn't got a turkey for dinner.'

'He can't produce turkeys out of a hat. What do you think he is—a magician? How can—'

'Oh, shut up, Wat. I don't know how he can get a turkey. That's his affair.'

'You expect too much. You may not have realised it yet, but there's a war on!'

Biggles, otherwise Captain Bigglesworth, eyed the recording officer sarcastically.

'Oh, there's a war on, is there?' he said. 'And you'd make that an excuse for not having turkey for Christmas dinner? I say it's all the more reason why we should have one. I'll bet every squadron on each side the Line has got turkey for dinner—except us!'

'Well, you're a bright boy,' returned Wat, 'why don't you go and get one, if it is so easy?'

'For two pins I'd do it!' snorted Biggles.

'Fiddlesticks!'

Biggles swung round on his heel.

'Fiddlesticks, my grandmother!' he snapped. 'Are you suggesting I couldn't get a turkey if I tried?'

'I am,' returned Wat. 'I know for a fact that Martin has ransacked every roost, shop and warehouse for a radius of fifty miles, and there isn't one to be had for love or money.'

'Oh!' Biggles said. 'Then in that case I shall have to see about getting one.'

Algy caught his eye and frowned.

'Don't make rash promises,' he said warningly.

'Well, when I do get one you'll be one of the first to line up with your plate, I'll be bound,' Biggles retorted. 'Look here, if I get the bird, will you all line up very respectfully and ask for a portion—and will somebody do my dawn patrols for a week?'

There was silence for a moment. Then:

'Yes, I will,' declared Mahoney.

'Good! You can be getting a stock of combat reports

ready, then,' declared Biggles, turning towards the door.

'Where are you off to?' called Wat.

'Turkey hunting,' replied Biggles shortly.

'And where do you imagine you are going to find one?'

'You don't suppose I'm going to stand here and wait for one to come and give itself up, do you? And you don't suppose I'm going to wander about this frost-bitten piece of landscape looking for one?' inquired Biggles coldly.

'But I tell you, you won't find a turkey within fifty miles!'

'That's all you know about it!' grunted Biggles, and went out and slammed the door.

Now, when that conversation had commenced, Biggles had not the remotest idea of where he was going to start his quest for a turkey. But presently something awakened in his memory. He had a clear recollection of seeing a large flock of turkeys below him on an occasion when he had been flying very low, and as he left the room to fulfil his rash promise he suddenly recalled where he had seen them.

He was half-way to the sheds when he called to mind the actual spot, and realised with dismay that it was over the other side of the Lines!

He paused in his stride and eyed the sky meditatively. The clouds were low, making reconnaissance-flying quite useless, but there were breaks through which a pilot who was willing to take chances might make his way to the 'sunny side'.

Returning to the ground would be definitely dangerous, for if the pilot chose to come down through the clouds at a spot where they reached to the ground, a crash would be inevitable. But once in the air the clouds would present plenty of cover. It was, in fact, the sort of day on which an enthusiastic airman might penetrate a good distance into enemy territory without encountering opposition.

He went on thoughtfully towards the sheds. The farm on which he had seen the turkeys, he remembered, was close to a village with a curiously shaped church tower. It was, to the best of his judgement, between thirty and forty miles over the Lines, and provided that the clouds were not absolutely solid in that region he felt confident of being able to find it again.

But he had by no means made up his mind to go, for the project bristled with big risks. To fly so far over enemy country alone was not a trip to be lightly undertaken. And to land in enemy territory and leave the machine—as he would have to do—was little short of madness. Was it worth the risk?

He decided it was not, and he was about to return to the mess when he was hailed by Algy and Mahoney, who had followed him up.

'Are you going turkey hunting in this atmosphere?' grinned Mahoney.

The remark was sufficient to cause Biggles to change his mind there and then, for he could stand anything except ridicule.

'Yes,' he said brightly, 'they fly very high, you know—higher than you ever go. But I think I can manage to bag one.'

'But you're not seriously thinking of flying?' cried Algy, aghast. 'It's impossible on a day like this! Look how low the clouds are!'

'You'll see whether I am or not,' muttered Biggles. 'Smyth, get my machine out.'

'But it—' began the N.C.O.

'Get it out—don't argue. My guns loaded?'

'Yes, sir.'

'Tanks full?'

'Yes, sir.'

'Then get it out and start up.'

'He's as mad as a March hare,' declared Mahoney hopelessly five minutes later, as Biggles' Camel plane roared up into the moisture-laden sky.

'He is!' agreed Algy. 'But it's time you knew him well enough to know that when he comes back he'll have a turkey with him—if he comes back at all.

'I wish I knew which way he'd gone. If I did I'd follow him to see that he doesn't get into mischief.'

After climbing swiftly through a hole in the clouds Biggles came out above them at five thousand feet, and after a swift but searching scrutiny of the sky turned his nose north-east. In all directions stretched a rolling sea of billowing mist that gleamed white in the wintry sun under a sky of blue.

North, south, east, and west he glanced in turn; but, as he expected, not a machine of any sort was in sight, and he settled himself down to his long flight hopefully. The first difficulty, he thought, would be to find and identify the village or farm; the next would be to land in a suitable field near at hand without damaging the machine.

He realised that his greatest chance of success lay in the fact that the place was so far over the Lines, well beyond the sphere of the German planes and the German infantry who were holding, or were in reserve for, the trenches. To have landed anywhere near them would have been suicidal.

As it was, his objective was a remote hamlet where the only opposition he was likely to encounter on the ground was a farmer, or his men, although there was always a chance of running into stray German troops

139

who were quartered or billeted well behind the Lines at rest camps, or on the lines of communication.

'Well, it's no use making plans on a job like this,' he mused. 'Let's find the place and see what happens.'

He glanced at his compass to make sure that he was on his course, and then at his watch, and noticed that he had been in the air nearly twenty-five minutes.

'Almost there,' he muttered, and began looking for a way down through the clouds. But in all directions they presented an unbroken surface, and, rather than risk over-shooting his objective, he throttled back, and, with his eyes on his altimeter, began gliding down through them.

He shivered involuntarily as the clammy mist closed about him and swirled around wings and fuselage like gale-blown smoke. Down—down—down; 3,000—2,000—1,000, and still there was no sign of the ground.

At five hundred feet, he was still in it, but it was getting thinner, and at three hundred feet he emerged over a sombre, snow-covered landscape. The country was absolutely strange to him, so he raced along just below the clouds, looking to right and left for a landmark that he could recognise.

For about five minutes he flew on, becoming more and more anxious, and he was beginning to think that he had made a big error of judgment, when straight ahead he saw the dim outline of a far-spreading wood. He recognised it at once.

'Dash it! I've come too far,' he muttered, and, turning the Camel in its own length, he began racing back over his course. 'There must be a following wind upstairs to take me as far over as this,' he mused as the minutes passed, and still he could see no sign of the village he sought.

He came upon it quite suddenly, and his heart gave

a leap as his eyes fell upon the well-remembered farm-house, with its rows of poultry houses. But where were the turkeys? Where was the flock of a hundred or more plump black birds that had fled so wildly at his approach on the last occasion? Then he understood.

'Of course!' he told himself savagely. 'What a fool I am! They're all dead by now. Plucked and hanging up in Berlin poulterers' shops, I expect. Ha!'

A sparkle came to his eyes as they fell on a great turkey cock, evidently the monarch of the flock, that had, no doubt, been kept as the leader of the next year's brood. It was standing outside one of the houses, with its feathers puffed out, its head on one side, and an eye cocked upwards on the invader of its domain.

'Don't stretch your neck, old cock; you'll have a closer view of me in a minute,' mumbled Biggles, as he took a quick glance around to get the lie of the land.

The poultry coops were in a small paddock about a hundred yards from the farmhouse and its outbuild-ings, which, in turn, were nearly a quarter of a mile from the village. There were several fields near at hand in which an aeroplane might be landed with some risk, and, as far as he could see, not a soul was in sight.

So much he was able to take in at a glance. There was no wood, or any other form of cover, so conceal-ment was out of the question. The raid would have to be made in the open and depend entirely upon speed for its success.

'Well, it's no use messing about,' he thought, and, cutting out his engine, glided down into a long, narrow field adjoining the paddock. He had a nasty moment or two as the machine bumped over the snow-covered tussocks and molehills with which the pasture was plen-tifully besprinkled; but, kicking on the right rudder just before the Camel ran to a standstill, he managed to swerve so that it stopped not far from the low hedge which divided the field from the paddock.

He was out of the cockpit at once and, with his eye on the farm, ran like a deer towards the turkey which still appeared to be watching the proceedings with the greatest interest.

It stood quite still until he was no more than ten yards away, but still on the wrong side of the hedge, and it was only when he began to surmount the obstacle that the turkey's interest began to take the form of mild alarm.

'Tch—tch!' clucked Biggles gently, holding out his hand and strewing the snow with imaginary grains of corn. But the bird was not so easily deluded. It began to sidestep away, wearing that air of offended dignity that only a turkey can adopt; and seeing that it was likely to take real fright at any moment, Biggles made a desperate leap.

But the turkey was ready; it sprang nimbly to one side, at the same time emitting a shrill gobble of alarm. Biggles landed on all fours in the sodden grass.

'I ought to have brought my gun for you,' he raged, 'and then I'd give you something to gobble about, you scraggy-necked—'

His voice died away as he gazed in stupefied astonishment at a man who had appeared at the door of the nearest poultry house—which, judging by the fork he held, he had been in the act of cleaning.

If Biggles was surprised, it was clear that the man was even more surprised, and for ten seconds they stared at each other speechlessly. Biggles was the first to recover his presence of mind, although he hesitated as to which course to pursue.

Remembering that he was in occupied Belgian territory, it struck Biggles that the man looked more like a Belgian than an enemy.

'Are you German?' Biggles asked sharply, in French.

'No, Belgian,' replied the other quickly. 'You are English, is it not?' he added quickly, glancing apprehensively towards the farmhouse.

The action was not lost on Biggles.

'Are those Germans in the house?' he asked tersely.

'Yes, the Boches are living in my house!' The Belgian spat viciously.

Biggles thought swiftly. If there were Germans in the house they would be soldiers, and, of course, armed. At any moment one of them might look out of a window and see him.

'Why have you come here?' the Belgian went on, in a nervous whisper.

Biggles pointed to the turkey.

'For that,' he answered.

# Chapter 17
# Biggles Gets the Bird

The Belgian looked at him in amazement. He looked at the bird, and then back at Biggles. Then he shook his head.

'That is impossible,' he said. 'I am about to kill it, for it has been kept back for the German officers in the village.'

'Will they pay you for it?' asked Biggles quickly.

'No.'

'Then I will. How much?'

The Belgian looked startled.

'It is not possible!' he exclaimed again.

'Isn't it?' Biggles cast a side-long glance at the turkey, which, reassured by the presence of the owner, whom it knew, was strutting majestically up and down within three yards of them. He thrust his hand into his pocket and pulled out some loose franc notes. 'Here, take this!' he said and leapt on to the bird.

This time there was no mistake, and he clutched it in both arms. He seized the flapping wings and held them together with his left hand, and took a firm grip of the neck with his right.

'Come on, kill it!' he called to the Belgian. 'I can't!'

There was a sudden shout from the direction of the house, and, looking up, he saw to his horror that a soldier in grey uniform was standing on the doorstep watching him. Again the call of alarm rang out, and a dozen or more German troops—some half-dressed, others fully clad and carrying rifles—poured out.

For a moment they stood rooted in astonishment, and then, in a straggling line, they charged down into the paddock.

Biggles waited for no more. Ducking under the outstretched arm of the farmer, who made a half-hearted attempt to stop him, he scrambled over the hedge into the field where he had left the machine. His foot caught in a briar, and he sprawled headlong; but the bird, which he had no intention of relinquishing, broke his fall, and he was up again at once.

Dishevelled, and panting with excitement, he sped towards the Camel. Fortunately, the impact of Biggles' ten stone weight as he fell seemed to have stunned the bird, or winded it; at any rate, it remained fairly passive during the dash to the machine.

As he ran, Biggles was wondering what he was going to do with the bird when he got to the aeroplane, and blamed himself for overlooking this very vital question. With time, he could have tied it to some part of the structure—the undercarriage, for instance—but with the Germans howling like a pack of hounds in full cry less than a hundred yards away, there was no time for that.

So he did the only thing possible. He slung the bird into the cockpit, and still holding it with his right hand climbed in after it. It was obvious at once that there was no room for both of them, for the cockpit of a Camel plane is small, and a turkey is a large bird.

At least, there was no room on the floor of the cockpit without jamming the control-stick one way or the other, which certainly would not do. The Camel was not fitted for side-by-side seating, so in sheer desperation he plonked the bird on to the seat and sat on it.

He felt sorry for the bird, but there was no alternative, and he mentally promised it respite as soon as they got clear of the ground.

A rifle cracked perilously near, and another, so without waiting to make any fine adjustments, he shoved the throttle open and sped across the snow. It did not take him long to realise that he had bitten off rather more than he could chew, for the turkey was not only a large bird, but a very strong one.

Whether it was simply recovering from the effects of the fall, or whether it was startled by the roar of the three hundred horse-power in the Camel's Bentley rotary engine, is neither here nor there; but the fact remains that no sooner had he started to take off than the bird gave a convulsive jerk that nearly threw him on to the centre section.

'Here, lie still!' he snarled, as he fought to keep his balance and keep the swinging Camel in a straight line. But the bird paid no heed, so in sheer desperation he pulled the machine off the ground and steered a crazy course into the sky.

He breathed a sigh of relief as his wheels lifted, for he had fully expected his undercarriage to buckle at any moment under the unusual strain. The danger of the troops being past, he attempted to adjust himself and his passenger into positions more conducive to safety and comfort.

He groped for his belt, but quickly discovered that its length—while suitably adapted for a single person—was not long enough to meet around him in his elevated position. So he abandoned it, and, keeping under the clouds, made for home, hoping that he would not find it necessary to fly in any other position than on even keel.

His head was, of course, sticking well up above the windscreen, and the icy slipstream of the propeller smote his face with hurricane force. He tried to crouch forward, but the turkey, relieved of part of his weight, seized the opportunity thus presented to make a commendable effort to return to its paddock.

It managed to get one wing in between Biggles' legs and, using it as a lever, nearly sent him over the side; he only saved himself by letting go of the control-stick and grabbing at the side of the cockpit with both hands. The machine responded at once to this unusual freedom by making a sickening swerving turn earthwards, and he only prevented a spin—which at that altitude would have been fatal—by the skin of his teeth.

'Phew!' he gasped, thoroughly alarmed. 'Another one like that and this bird'll have the cockpit to himself!' He brought the machine on an even keel, at the same time taking a swift look around for possible trouble.

He saw it at once, in the shape of a lone Albatross scout that had evidently just emerged from the clouds, and was now moving towards him.

He pursed his lips, then automatically bent forward to see if his gun sight was in order; only then did he realise that he was much too high in his seat to get his eye anywhere near it. In a vain attempt to do this he again crouched forward, and once more the bird displayed its appreciation of the favour by heaving to such good purpose that Biggles was flung forwards so hard that his nose struck the top edge of the windscreen.

He blinked under the blow, and retaliated by fetching the cause of it a smart jab with his left elbow.

Meanwhile, the Hun was obviously regarding the unusual position and antics of the pilot with deep suspicion, for he half turned away before approaching warily from another direction.

147

'That fellow must think I've got St Vitus' Dance,' thought Biggles moodily, as the bird started a new movement of short, sharp jerks which had the effect of causing the pilot to bob up and down and the machine to pursue a curious, undulating course.

'My hat, I don't wonder he's scared!' he concluded. 'Oh, my goodness!'

The turkey had at last succeeded in getting its head free, and it raised it aloft to a point not a foot from Biggles' face; the look of dignity it had once worn was now replaced by one of surprise and disapproval.

For a moment or two all went well, for the bird seemed to be satisfied with this modicum of freedom, and began to look from side to side at its unusual surroundings with considerable interest.

'Yes, my lad, that's a Hun over there!' Biggles told it viciously, as the Albatross swept round behind them. 'If you start playing the fool again you're likely to be roasted with your feathers on!'

Taka-taka-taka-taka! Biggles saw that the Hun had placed himself in a good position for attack, and he knew that the matter was getting serious. He had no intention of losing his life for the sake of a meal, so he forthwith prepared to jettison his cargo—an action which had always been in the background of his mind as a last resort.

But, to his increasing alarm, he found that this was going to be a by no means simple matter, and he was considering the best way of accomplishing it when the staccato chatter of machine-guns, now very close, reached his ears.

To stunt, or even return the attack, was out of the question, and, now, thoroughly alarmed, he moved his body as far forward as possible in order to allow the bird to wriggle up behind him and escape. The turkey appeared to realise his intention, and began worming its way upward between his back and the seat.

Taka-taka-taka-taka-taka!

'Get out, you fool!' yelled Biggles as he heard the bullets boring into the fuselage behind him; but either the bird did not understand or else it refused to accept his invitation, for it remained quite still. There was only one thing to do, and he did it. He pulled the control-stick back and shot upwards into the clouds.

To climb right through them—a distance of, perhaps, several thousand feet—was, of course, impossible, for to keep the machine level in such conditions was out of the question.

Still, he hung on as long as he could, until, finding himself becoming giddy, he dived earthward again, and looked anxiously for his pursuer as he emerged into clear air.

To his annoyance, he saw that the Hun was still there, about three hundred yards behind him.

In turning to look behind he had put his left hand on the bird, and as he turned once more he saw, to his horror, that his glove was covered with blood.

'I've been hit!' was his first thought.

Then he grasped the true state of affairs. No wonder the bird was quiet—it was dead.

It had stopped the burst of fire which in normal circumstances would have caught him—Biggles—in the small of the back!

The shock sobered him, but he found that it was a good deal easier to dispose of a dead bird than a living one. Twenty-odd pounds of dead weight was a very different proposition to the same weight of jerking, flapping, muscular life, and he had no difficulty in stowing it in the space between the calves of his legs and the bottom of the seat.

This done, he quickly buckled his safety-belt, and, turning to his attacker, saw, to his intense satisfaction, that, presumably encouraged by his opponent's disinclination to fight, the Hun was coming in carelessly to deliver the knock-out.

Biggles spun the Camel round in its own length and shot up in a clear, climbing turn that brought him behind the straight-winged machine. That the pilot had completely lost him he saw at a glance, for he had raised his head from his sights, and was looking up and down, as if bewildered by the Camel's miraculous disappearance.

Confidently Biggles roared down to point-blank range. The German looked round over his shoulder at the same moment, but he was too late, for Biggles' hand had already closed over his gun-lever.

He fired only a short burst, but it was enough. The Albatross reared up on its tail, fell off on to a wing, and then spun earthwards, its engine roaring in full throttle.

He did not wait to see it crash. He was more concerned with getting home, for he was both cold and tired. He found a rift in the clouds, climbed up through it, and, without seeing a machine of any description, crossed the lines into comparative safety.

Judging the position of the aerodrome as well as he could, he crept cautiously back to the ground, and landed on the deserted tarmac.

With grim satisfaction, he hauled the corpse of his unwitting preserver from the cockpit, and, flinging it over his shoulder, strode towards the mess.

It struck him that the bird had increased in weight, and he wondered at the reason until he recalled the length of the Hun's burst of firing, and deduced that most of the bullets, which had been partly arrested by

150

the structure of the machine, must even now be reposing in the carcass that dangled over his back.

A moment of dead silence greeted him as he opened the mess door, and, still in his flying-kit, heaved the body of his feathered passenger on to the table. Then a babble of voices broke out.

Mahoney pushed his way to the front, staring.

'Where on earth did you get that?' he cried incredulously.

'I told you I was going turkey hunting,' replied Biggles simply, 'and—well, there you are! Look a bit closer, and you'll see the bullet-holes. I don't like reminding you, old lad, but don't forget you're doing my early patrols next week.

'And, finally, don't forget I'm carving the turkey!' he laughed.

# Chapter 18
# A Sporting Offer!

The healthy, boyish face of the Hon. Algernon Lacey, of Squadron No. 266, wore a remarkable expression, as its owner walked in long strides towards the officers' mess from the direction of the squadron office.

He hesitated in his stride, as Maclaren, the doughty Scots flight-commander, emerged from his hut, cap in hand, and stared thoughtfully at the sky.

'Hi, Mac!' hailed Algy. 'Have you seen Biggles anywhere?'

'Ay. He's in the billiards-room.'

'Thanks!' Algy hurried on, entered the mess, crossed the ante-room, and pushed open the door of the room in which a small billiards-table had been installed.

'Enter the gallant knight, Sir Algernon!' chaffed Biggles, who was sitting in a cane chair with his feet resting on the window-sill, with a small circle of officers around him.

'Hi!' cried Algy. 'I've some news that will shake you!'

'You may have news, but I doubt it will shake me,' rejoined Biggles. 'I've been in this perishing war too long for anything to occasion me either surprise or consternation. What is it? Has Fishface decided to stand us a dinner?'

Fishface was the popular name for Brigadier-General Tishlace, general officer commanding the wing in which Squadron No. 266 was brigaded.

'No,' replied Algy; 'at least, not as far as I know. But Wat Tyler has just shown me tonight's orders—

they're being typed now. We've been detailed for a week's propaganda work. Several other units have got to do it, too, I believe.'

'Propaganda?'

'Yes. You know the game—dropping leaflets over the other side of the line telling the Huns that they're losing the war, and if they like to be good boys and give themselves up, what a lovely time they'll have in England!'

'Great Scott! What will they want us to do next? Do they think we're a lot of unemployed postmen?'

'It's no joking matter,' answered Algy seriously. 'D'you know what the Huns do to people they catch at this game?'

'No. But I can guess.'

'It's either a firing-party at dawn, up against a brick wall, or the salt mines in Siberia!'

'Then, obviously, the thing is not to get caught.'

'You've said it,' observed Mahoney. 'I had to do this job once when I was in Squadron 96. We didn't go far over the Line, I can tell you; in fact, Billy Bradley dropped a load only about two miles over.

'There was a dickens of a wind blowing at the time, and it blew the whole lot back over the aerodrome. It looked as if the whole blooming Army had been having a paperchase!'

'How do you drop em?' asked Biggles curiously.

'They're done up in bundles, with an elastic band round them. You just pull the band off and heave the whole packet over the side. They separate as they fall, and look like an artificial snowstorm at a pantomime.'

'Well,' declared Biggles, 'I don't mind a rough-house once in a while, but I'd hate to dig salt in Siberia. I never did like salt, anyway. When do we start this jaunt?'

'Tomorrow morning.'

The door was flung open, and Wilkinson—better known as 'Wilks,' of the neighbouring S.E. 5 Squadron—entered, and broached the object of his visit without delay.

'I hear you blighters have been detailed for this paperchase to-morrow?'

'So Algy says,' replied Biggles. 'Why, what do you know about it?'

'We've been doing it for the last three days.'

'The dickens you have!'

'We have. And we're pretty good at it!'

'How do you mean good? It doesn't strike me that it needs any great mental effort to throw a bundle of papers over the side of an aeroplane. Still, it's the sort of thing your crowd might easily learn to do quite well.'

'Don't you make any mistake! Headquarters usually has a job to make people go far over the line, but we're doing the job properly. I dropped a load over Lille yesterday.'

'Lille! But you don't call that far. It's only about ten miles!'

'It's far enough, and further than you Camel merchants are likely to go!'

Biggles rose slowly to his feet.

'We'll see about that!' he declared. 'I should say that where a palsied, square-faced S.E. plane can go, a Camel should have no difficulty in going. In fact, it could probably go a bit further.

'In order to prove it, tomorrow I shall make a point of heaving a load of this confetti over Tournai.'

'You're barmy!' jeered Wilks. 'How are you going to prove you've been there, anyway?'

'If you're going to start casting nasturtiums at my integrity, I shall have to take a camera—'

He broke off, and with the other officers rose to his feet as Major Raymond, of Wing Headquarters Intelligence Staff, entered the room with Major Mullen, the C.O.

'Good-morning, gentlemen!' said the Wing officer. 'All right, sit down, everybody. What were you talking about, Bigglesworth? Did I hear you say you were going to heave something at somebody?'

'Yes, sir,' replied Biggles. 'Wilks here—Wilkinson—says he dropped a packet of these—er—propaganda leaflets over Lille yesterday. Just to show that there was no ill-feeling, I said I'd drop a load over at Tournai.'

'Tournai! It's a long way—about thirty miles, I should say, for a guess. I should be glad to see you do it, but it's taking a big risk.'

'No distance at all, sir. I thought it might be a good thing if we set Wilks and his S.E.5 people a mark to aim at. Shackleton's Farthest South sort of thing—or, rather, Farthest East.'

Major Raymond smiled.

'I see,' he said slowly. 'If your C.O. has no objection, I'll tell you what I'll do. I'll present a new gramophone to the squadron that takes a packet of those leaflets Farthest East during the next two days.

'Time expires—shall we say—at twelve noon the day after tomorrow?'

'That's very sporting of you, sir!' replied Biggles. 'You might order a label made out to Squadron No. 266—'

'You wait a minute,' broke in Wilkinson. 'Not so fast!' Then he turned to Major Raymond. 'You make the label out to us, sir; it will save you altering it.'

'I think I'll wait for the result first!' laughed the major. 'I shall expect a photograph for proof, and I shall be outside, on the Tarmac, at twelve o'clock the day after tomorrow, to check up. Good-bye!'

Biggles bent forward and peered through the arc of his whirling propeller for the fiftieth time, and examined the sky carefully. Satisfied that it was clear, he turned and looked long and searchingly over his shoulder.

From horizon to horizon not a speck marked the unbroken blue of the sky.

He glanced at his watch and saw that he had been in the air rather more than an hour. Thirty minutes of it he had spent in climbing to his limit of height over his own side of the Lines, and for the remainder of the time he had pushed further and further into hostile country.

It was the day following the discussion in the mess, and, in accordance with his declared intention, he had left the ground shortly after dawn, bound for Tournai.

So far he had been fortunate, for he had not seen a single machine of any sort. Even the archie had dwindled away as he had penetrated beyond the usual scene of operations.

Below lay a rolling landscape of green fields and woods, very different from that nearer the Lines. It was new to him, for although he had been as far over on one or two previous occasions, it had not been in this actual area.

Again he peered ahead, and saw that his course had been correct. Tournai, a broad splash of grey, red and brown walls, lay athwart the landscape, like an island in a dream sea.

He wiped the frosted air from his windscreen, unwrapped a piece of chocolate from its silver jacket, and popped it into his mouth, and once more began his systematic scrutiny of the atmosphere. The sky was still clear.

'It looks as if it's going to be easy!' he thought as he took a camera from the pocket in the side of his cockpit and placed it on his lap.

Then he groped under the cushion on which he sat and produced the object of the raid.

It was a tightly packed wad of thin paper, not unlike banknotes, held together by an elastic band.

Once more he searched the sky. Satisfied that he had nothing to fear, he eased the control-stick forward for more speed, and roared across his objective.

When he was slightly to the windward side of it, he took his unusual missile from his lap, pulled off the elastic band, and flung it over the side.

Instantly the swirling slipstream tore the papers apart and scattered them far and wide. By the time he turned for home, a vast multitude of what appeared to be small white moths were floating slowly earthward.

It was an extraordinary spectacle, and a smile came to his face as he watched it.

Then he turned, to bring the sun behind him, aimed his camera at the scene below, and depressed the shutter release. He repeated the process, in case of an accident occurring to one of the plates, and then raced away towards the distant Lines.

Twenty minutes passed, and only half the distance had been covered, for he was now flying against a headwind. Nevertheless, he had just begun to hope that he would reach home without being molested, when a cluster of fine dots appeared over the western horizon.

The effect was not unlike a small swarm of gnats on a summer's evening. He altered his course slightly to make a detour round them, but continued to watch them closely. The speed with which they increased in

157

size made it clear that the machines were travelling in his direction, and presently he could make them out distinctly.

It was the formation of six British bombers, D.H. 4's, being hotly attacked on all sides by some fifteen or twenty Albatross scouts. The D.H.'s seemed to be holding their own, however, and held on their way, flying in a tight V-formation.

The affair was nothing to do with Biggles; in any case, he could not hope to serve any good purpose by butting in, although he wondered why no escort had been provided for the bombers, so he gave them as wide a berth as possible, hoping to pass unobserved. But it was not to be.

First one of the enemy scouts saw him, then another, until the air between him and the D.H. 4's was filled with a long line of gaudily painted aeroplanes, all racing in his direction.

'Those "4" pilots ought to be pleased with me,' he thought bitterly, 'for taking that mob off their heels. This is going to be awkward!'

The Albatrosses were at about his own altitude; if anything, they were a trifle higher, which gave them a slight advantage of speed. To fight such a crowd successfully, so far from home, once they had drawn level with him, was obviously impossible.

He was, as near as he could judge, still a good twelve miles over the enemy's side of the Lines, not a great distance as distance counts on the ground, but a long way when one is fighting against overwhelming odds.

He looked around for a cloud in which he might take cover, or around which he might dodge his pursuers, but in all directions the sky was clear. He scanned the horizon anxiously, hoping to see some of the scouts of his own side with whom he could join until the danger was past, but the only British machines in sight were the fast disappearing D.H. 4's.

The nearest Albatross was less than a quarter of a mile away. Once it caught him he would be compelled to stay and fight, for to fly straight on would mean being shot down like a sparrow.

'Well, I'll get as near home as I can before we start,' he thought, pushing the control-stick forward. The note of the engine, augmented by the scream of the wind round wires and struts, increased in volume as the Camel plunged downwards.

Biggles flew with his head twisted round over his shoulder, watching his pursuers, and as the leader drew within range he kicked the rudder-bar and threw the Camel into a spin, from which he did not pull out until he was as near the ground as he dare go.

He came out facing the direction of the Lines, and although the Albatrosses had spun with him, as he knew they would, he managed to make another two or three miles before they came up to him again.

The combat could no longer be postponed, yet if he stayed to fight so far from home, the end was inevitable.

However many machines he shot down, in the end his turn would come, for the longer he fought, the more enemy machines would arrive. A large field lay almost immediately under him, and a little further on he saw an aerodrome, and an idea flashed into his head, although he had no time to ponder on it.

The vicious rattle of a machine-gun reached his ears, warning him that the Hun leader was already within range. He jerked the control-stick back and sideslipped earthwards, imitating as nearly as he could the actions of a pilot who had been badly hit. Would it work? He could but try.

Following his plan, he swerved low over the treetops, throttled back, and ran to a standstill at the far side of the big field, after steering an erratic course. Then he sagged forward in the cockpit and remained still.

Out of the corner of his eye he watched the many-hued torpedo-like Albatrosses circling above him. An orange-coloured machine, the one that had fired at him, detached itself from the others and glided down to land.

One by one the remainder turned over the hedge and made for the aerodrome, from which a party was no doubt on its way to take charge of the wounded 'prisoner'.

Biggles sat quite still, with his engine idling, as the orange Hun taxied towards him. At a distance of about twenty yards the pilot stopped, switched off his engine, jumped to the ground, and walked quickly towards the Camel.

Biggles waited until only half a dozen paces divided them, and then he sat upright, and the German stopped dead as he found himself staring into the smiling face of the British pilot, the German obviously undecided as to whether he should come on or go back.

Like most pilots, he was probably unarmed, but Biggles was taking no unnecessary risks. His plan had so far materialised, and he lost no time in carrying it to completion.

He raised his hand in salute to the astonished German, blipped his engine derisively, and then sped across the turf at ever increasing speed.

He cleared the hedge on the far side, tore across the German aerodrome with his wheels only a foot or two from the ground, and still keeping as low as possible, set his nose for home.

On the far side of the aerodrome he saw the German

pilots, who had left their machines, running back to them and others taxi-ing to get head into wind; but he was not alarmed.

In the minute or two that would elapse before they could take up the trail again, he would get a clear lead of two miles, a flying start that the Germans could never make up!

And so it transpired. The Camel came under a certain amount of rifle fire from the troops on the ground, both in the reserve trenches and the front Line, but as far as Biggles knew not a single bullet touched the machine.

Ten minutes later he landed at Maranique, where the C.O. and several officers, were apparently awaiting his return.

Major Mullen threw a quick glance over the Camel as Biggles climbed out, camera in hand.

'You didn't have much trouble, I see!' he observed.

'No, sir,' replied Biggles coolly. 'I didn't find it necessary to fire a shot.'

'Did you get your photo?'

'I think so, sir. I should like it developed as soon as possible—Wilks might like to have a copy of it.'

'Here's a letter for you from Wilks,' said Wat Tyler, passing him a large square envelope. 'A motor-cyclist brought it to the Squadron Office just after you took off.'

Biggles looked at the envelope suspiciously, then tore it open, and from it he withdrew a whole-plate photograph. It was an oblique picture, and showed a fairly large town, but it was half obscured by what seemed to be hundreds of small white specks that ran diagonally across it, just as his own leaflets had appeared above Tournai. A frown creased his forehead.

'Can anybody recognise this place?' he said sharply.

Major Mullen took the photograph, looked at it for a moment, and then turned it over.

'Ah!' he said. 'I thought so! It's Gontrude, taken from eighteen thousand feet. He must have taken the photograph yesterday, after he left here.'

'Where's Gontrude?' asked Biggles slowly. 'I don't remember ever seeing it.'

'No, it's rather a long way over,' replied Major Mullen, with a curious smile. 'It's about twelve miles the other side of Tournai, I fancy.'

Biggles staggered back and sat down suddenly on a chock.

'Well, the dirty dog!' he exclaimed. 'So I've been all the way to Tournai for nothing!'

'It rather looks like it,' agreed the major sympathetically.

'So Wilks thinks he's being funny, does he?' muttered Biggles. 'Well, we shall see! There's another day left yet!' and he strode off towards the mess.

# Chapter 19
# Getting a Gramophone

Later in the day Biggles called Algy over to him.

'Look, laddie,' he said, 'I've been exercising my mental equipment on this crazy long-distance stunt, and the points that stick out most clearly in my mind are these:

'First of all, if it goes on, somebody's going to get killed; it's asking for trouble.

'Secondly, we can't let Wilks and his crowd get away with it. Hitherto, we've always managed to put it across them, so if they pull this off they'll crow all the louder.

'If they get the gramophone, they'll play it every guest night, and everyone for miles will know what it means.

'I made a mistake in telling Wilks that I was going to Tournai, because then he knew just how far he had to go to beat me. The way I see it is this—it's no use doddering about just going another five miles, and another five miles, and so on—apart from anything else it's too risky.

'We've got to do one more show, and it's got to be such a whizzer that Wilks will never suspect it. At the same time, it is no use risking running out of petrol on the wrong side of the Line—that would be just plain foolishness.'

Algy looked at him knowingly.

'You've got an idea under your hat,' he said shrewdly. 'What is it? Come on, cough it up!'

'You're right,' admitted Biggles, 'I have. I'm thinking of going to—come here.' He caught Algy by the arm and whispered in his ear.

Algy started violently.

'You must be off your rocker!' he exclaimed. 'You'd run out of petrol for a certainty. The only way you could possibly do it would be by taking straight off over the Lines without climbing for any height, and then the Huns would see to it that you didn't get there. No—'

'Shut up a minute,' said Biggles, 'and let me say my little piece! D'you suppose I haven't thought of all that! I'm out to put it across Wilks, but I've no intention of having my bright young life nipped in the bud for any measly gramophone.

'To start on such a show by flying low over the Lines would be like putting your head into the lion's mouth and expecting it not to bite. The higher the start, the better.

'The danger lies near the Lines—not fifty miles beyond them, where they'd no more expect to see a Camel than an extinct brontosaurus. I should climb to 18,000 feet over this side, while it is still dark, so that I couldn't be seen, and aim to be forty miles over the other side by the time it began to get light.

'It would be a thousand to one against meeting a Hun there, particularly at that height, and it is unlikely that I should be spotted from the ground.'

'But if you had to climb to that height at the start you wouldn't have anything like enough petrol to—'

'Wait a minute—let me finish. That's where you come in!'

Algy frowned.

'Me!' he exclaimed. 'So I'm in this, am I?'

'You wouldn't like to be left out, would you?' murmured Biggles reprovingly.

Algy regarded him suspiciously.

'Go ahead!' he said. 'What do you want me to do?'

At eleven-thirty the following morning, the aerodrome at Maranique presented an animated appearance, for rumours of the contest had leaked out, and pilots had come from nearby squadrons to see the conclusion.

The S.E.5 pilots of Squadron No. 287 were there in force, as was only to be expected. Major Mullen, looking a trifle worried, was talking to Major Raymond, who had just arrived in his car.

Wilks had not yet turned up, and Biggles was conspicuous by his absence, a fact which caused a good deal of vague speculation, for although certain other officers had aspired to win the prize in the earlier stages of the contest, they had soon abandoned their ideas before the suicidal achievements of the two chief participants, Biggles and Wilks.

Algy came out of the mess and made his way towards the crowd on the tarmac, to be bombarded with the question: 'Where's Biggles?' He looked tired, and there was a large smear of oil across his chin; he turned a deaf ear to the question.

'Where have you been?' asked an S.E.5 pilot suspiciously.

'What's that got to do with you?' retorted Algy. 'Where's Wilks, anyway?'

As if in answer to the question, all eyes turned upwards as an S.E.5 roared into sight over the far side of the aerodrome; it pulled up steeply into a spectacular climbing turn, side-slipped vertically, and made a neat tarmac landing.

Wilks, his face beaming, stepped out holding in his hand a sheet of paper which, as he approached, could be seen to be a photograph. He walked straight up to

Major Raymond, saluted, and handed the photograph to him.

'That is my final entry for the competition, sir,' he announced.

The major returned the salute, and looked at the photograph.

'Where is this?' he asked.

'Mons, sir.'

A cheer broke from the S.E.5 pilots, for at that period Mons was between fifty and sixty miles inside German occupied territory.

'Well, that will take some beating,' admitted the major, amid renewed cheers.

He looked around the sky.

Where was Biggles? He wondered.

As a matter of fact, Biggles was not quite sure himself. He knew vaguely, but cloud interference had blotted out the earth, and although he caught occasional glimpses of it from time to time, he had found it impossible to pick up the landmarks he had followed on the outward journey.

As in the case of his raid on Tournai, he had reached his objective with ridiculous ease, and had turned his back on it half an hour previously, but against the everlasting prevailing west wind he was still, according to his reckoning, some forty miles from the Lines.

That they were likely to prove the hardest part of his trip he was well aware, for even if his presence over the objective had not been reported to German headquarters by ground observers, his passage would have been noted by hostile air units, who would climb to the limit of their height to await his return.

He had realised that this was inevitable, and although he had given the matter a lot of thought he was still unable to make up his mind whether it would be better to stay where he was—at 18,000 feet—or go right down to the ground and hedge-hop home, when there might be a chance of evading the watching eyes above.

Although what he gained on the swings he was likely to lose on the roundabouts, for at a very low altitude he would come under the fire of all arms—machine-guns, anti-aircraft guns, flaming onions,* and even field-guns.

He peered ahead through his centre section struts with searching intensity, and then drew a deep breath.

Far away—so far that only the keenest eyes could have detected them—were three groups of tiny black specks. They stretched right across his course, and not for an instant did he attempt to delude himself as to what they were.

So far from the Lines, they could mean only one thing—hostile aircraft; German scouts in formation.

He moistened his lips, pushed up his goggles, and looked down. It was the only way. Quickly but coolly he made up his mind, and acted simultaneously. He retarded his fine adjustment throttle, and as the noise of the engine died away he deliberately allowed the machine to stall, at the same time kicking on the right rudder.

The Camel needed no further inducement to spin. In an instant it was plunging earthward, rotating viciously about its longitudinal axis—the dreaded right-hand spin that had sent so many Camel pilots to their deaths.

But Biggles knew his machine, and although he was temporarily out of control he could recover it when he chose.

He allowed the spin to persist until the fields below

* Slang: a type of incendiary anti-aircraft shell used only by the Germans.

167

became a whirling disc; then he pulled out and spun in the reverse direction.

The spin was not quite so fast, but he pulled out feeling slightly giddy and flew level, to allow his altimeter to adjust itself, for in his rush earthwards he had overtaken it, losing height faster than the needle could indicate it.

'Six thousand!' he muttered.

In a minute of time he had spun off twelve thousand feet of height!

He warmed his engine again, side-slipping as he did so in order to continue to lose height. The wind howled through his rigging, and a blast of air struck him on the right cheek. He tilted the machine over to the right, control-stick right over, applying opposite rudder to keep his nose up and prevent the machine from stalling.

These tactics he continued until he was less than a hundred feet from the ground; then, with throttle wide open, he raced, tail up, for the Lines, leaning far back in the cockpit to enable him to command a wide view overhead.

A cloud of white smoke, from which radiated long, white pencil-lines, blossomed out in front of him, and he altered his course slightly.

'Dash it!' he muttered. It was no time for half-measures. Lower and lower he forced the Camel, until his wheels were just skimming above the ground.

Only by flying below the limit of the trajectory of that gun could he hope to baffle the gunners.

On, on between trees and over scattered homesteads he roared in the maddest ride of his life. Cattle stampeded before him, poultry flapped wildly aside, and field labourers flung themselves flat before the demon that hurtled towards them like a thunderbolt.

All the time he was getting nearer home, raising his

eyes every few seconds to watch the enemy machines overhead.

Five minutes passed—ten—fifteen, and then a grim smile spread over his face.

'They've spotted me!' he muttered. 'Here they come!' He glanced at his watch. 'About five miles to go. They'll catch me, but with luck I might just do it!'

A wide group of many-hued bodies were falling from the sky ahead of him, but he did not alter his course a fraction of an inch, although he flinched once or twice as he tore past flashing wings and whirling propellers. He heard the rattle of guns behind him, but he did not stop to return the fire.

'Out of my way!' he snarled as a fresh formation appeared in front of him. 'Turn, or I'll ram—Oh!' He caught his breath as an Albatross shot past his nose, missing him by inches.

A bunch of Fokker Triplanes tore into his path, but as if sensing the berserk madness of the lone pilot, they prudently swung aside to let him through.

He tilted his wing to enable him to clear a church spire that suddenly appeared in his path, and then twisted violently the other way to avoid a tall poplar. He snatched a swift glance behind him, and his eyes opened wide.

'What a sight!' he gasped. 'Well, come on, boys; I'll take you for a joy-ride!'

A sudden hush fell on the crowd on the tarmac at Maranique as the drone of a Bentley rotary engine was borne on the breeze, and all eyes turned upwards to where a Camel could be seen approaching the aerodrome.

Over the edge of the aerodrome the engine choked, choked again, and back-fired. The prop stopped, and the nose of the machine tilted down. The watchers held their breath as it became apparent that the Camel was in difficulties.

A long strip of fabric trailed back from the wing-tip, and a bracing wire hung loose from the under-carriage; one of the ailerons* seemed to be out of position, as if it was hanging on by a single hinge.

There was silence as the pilot made a slow, flat turn that brought him into the wind, and then sagged earthwards like a drunken man. A few feet from the ground he caught it again, and flopped down to a bumpy landing.

A sigh of relief, like the rustle of dead leaves on an autumn day, broke from the spectators as the tension was relaxed.

Algy had started running towards the machine, but pulled up as Biggles was seen climbing from the cockpit. In his hand be carried a camera.

A mechanic of the photographic staff ran out to meet him as if by arrangement, and relieved him of the instrument. Biggles walked slowly on towards the group, removing his cap and goggles as he came.

He was rather pale, and looked very tired, but there was a faint smile about the corners of his mouth. He changed his direction slightly as he saw Major Raymond and made towards him.

'Sorry, sir, but I shall have to keep you a minute or two until my photograph is developed,' he said. 'But I've still got another quarter of an hour or so, I think?'

The major looked at his wrist-watch.

'Fourteen minutes,' he said. Then his curiosity overcame him. 'Where have you been?' he inquired, with interest.

* Usually a part of the trailing edge of a wing, used to turn the aircraft to left or right by means of the control column.

170

'I should prefer not to say, sir, if you don't mind, until the photo arrives.'

'Just as you like.'

Ten minutes passed slowly, and then Flight-Sergeant Smyth appeared, running towards the crowd with a broad smile on his face. He handed something to Biggles, who, after a swift glance, passed it to the major.

'Where is this?' said the staff officer, with a puzzled expression. 'I seem to recognise those buildings.'

'Brussels, sir.'

'Brussels?' cried Wilks. 'I don't believe it! You couldn't carry enough petrol to get to Brussels and back!'

'Whether he could or not, this is a photograph of Brussels,' declared the major. 'And there are leaflets fluttering down over the Palais Royal. I can see them distinctly.'

A yell from the Camel pilots split the air, while the S.E. pilots muttered amongst themselves.

'But how on earth did you do it?' cried the C.O. in amazement.

'Ah, that's a trade secret, sir!' replied Biggles mysteriously. 'But I am going to tell you, because it is only fair to Lacey, whose assistance made it possible. We flew over together, and landed in a field about forty miles over the Line.

'He carried eight spare tins of petrol—four in his cockpit and four lashed to his bomb-racks. He came back home; I refuelled and went on. I had just enough petrol to get back, as you saw.'

'But that isn't fair!' muttered Wilks.

'Oh, yes, it is!' said the major quickly. 'There was no stipulation about refuelling.'

'Do we get the gramophone, sir?' asked Biggles.

'You do!' replied the major promptly, and he handed it over.

Wilks' face broke into a smile, and he extended his hand.

'Good show, Biggles!' he said. 'You deserve it!'

'Thanks!' smiled Biggles. 'How about you and your chaps coming over to dinner tonight? We'll have a merry evening, with a tune on the jolly old gramophone to wind up with!'

For a moment Wilks looked doubtful, as though the mention of the gramophone gave him a nasty taste in the mouth. Then Biggles saw a sudden gleam flash into his eyes and a smile break out on his face

'Right-ho!' said Wilks. 'We'll be along. Thanks very much!' And he swung away in the direction of his plane, followed by the rest of his squadron.

'H'm!' grunted Biggles, as he watched him depart. 'If I'm not mistaken, you mean mischief. I'll have to keep a wary eye on you, my lad!'

When Wilks turned up for dinner that night, only half his fellow-pilots were with him.

'Hallo!' said Biggles, as Wilks and his comrades walked into the ante-room, where the newly won gramophone was playing a lively tune. 'Where's the rest of your chaps? We expect you all!'

'They couldn't get away,' explained Wilkinson.

'Hard luck!' said Biggles. 'Can't be helped, I suppose. Well, come along—dinner's ready.' And he led the way into the mess.

Dinner was a merry affair. It seemed as though the visiting pilots were out to prove that no trace of soreness over their defeat in the gramophone contest remained. Good-natured banter was exchanged, and the room was in a constant uproar of laughter.

It seemed to Biggles that at times the laughter of

the S.E.5 pilots was a trifle forced—as if they were deliberately making a noise to drown out other possible noises, and he chuckled inwardly. And he chuckled still more when he noticed Wilks taking furtive glances at his wrist-watch.

Suddenly Wilks noticed that Algy was not present, and he asked after him.

'Oh,' said Biggles casually, 'he's got a stunt on I—'

He broke off as a sudden uproar came from the ante-room, and, pushing back his chair, he leapt for the door. Thrusting it open, he dashed out into a group of figures milling round the gramophone.

In the midst of the group was Algy, gallantly defending the gramophone, holding off the S.E.5 pilots who had failed to turn up for dinner.

'Two-sixty-six to the rescue!' yelled Biggles, dashing into the fray.

In a moment the affair was over as other pilots of No. 266 Squadron dashed to the rescue.

'So this was Algy's stunt!' said the crestfallen Wilks bitterly.

'It was!' chuckled Biggles. 'And it's the winning stunt! It's no good, my lad,' he added. 'If you want a new gramophone you'll have to buy one. We won this, and we're jolly well keeping it!'

# Chapter 20
# Twelve Thousand Feet Up!

The aerodrome of Squadron No. 266 was deserted, except for a slim figure that sat, rather uncomfortably, on an upturned chock, as a Sopwith Camel, considerably damaged, landed and taxied up to the hangars — for officers and air mechanics were in their respective messes eating the midday meal.

The pilot of the Camel plane, Biggles, alighted slowly and deliberately. He removed the tangled remains of a pair of goggles from his head, shook some loose glass from the creases of his flying-jacket, and eyed a long tear in the arm of the garment dubiously.

Then be bent and examined the sole of his flying boot, the heel of which appeared to have been dragged off. Apparently satisfied with his inspection, he took a soiled handkerchief from his pocket and carefully wiped away a quantity of black oil from the lower part of his face.

This done, he thrust the handkerchief back in his pocket and glanced sideways at Algy Lacey, who had deserted his seat in front of the sheds, and was inspecting the much-shot-about aeroplane from various angles.

'You seem to have been having some fun,' suggested Algy.

'Fun, eh?' grunted Biggles, pointing to the shot-torn machine. 'If that's your idea of fun, it's time you were locked up in a padded cell!'

'All right, don't get the heebie-jeebies!'

'You'd have the screaming willies—never mind the heebie-jeebies—if you'd been with me this morning. Where's everybody?'

'At lunch.'

'That's all some people think of! If they'd do less guzzling and more— But why talk about it? Come on, let's go! I'll ring up Smyth from the mess to get busy on this kite!'

'Where've you been? You seem peeved about something,' observed Algy, as they made their way to the dining-room.

'If thirty Huns wouldn't peeve anybody, I should like to know what would!'

'Hallo, Biggles!' called Mahoney, from the lower end of the long trestle-table. 'Where've you been?'

'Ah, here's another wants to know all about it!' replied Biggles. 'All right, I'll tell you. I'm going to knock the block off that hound Wilkinson!'

'All right—all right, don't get het up! What's he done now?'

Biggles seated himself with slow deliberation, ordered cold beef from the mess waiter, and reached for the salad. He selected a tomato and stabbed it viciously. A small jet of pink spray squirted from it and struck Maclaren, the Scots flight-commander, in the eye.

Maclaren rose wrathfully to his feet, groping for his serviette.

'Here, what's the big idea?' he spluttered.

'Sorry, Mac,' murmured Biggles apologetically. 'But how did I know it was so juicy?'

'Well, look what you're doing!'

'Right-ho! As I was saying—where did I get to? Oh, yes! Well, this morning, on my way out to the Line, I thought I'd drop in and have a word with Wilks and thank him for sending down that bunch of records for the new gramophone.

'When I got there I found them all in a rare state. It seems that the old Boeleke "circus," which has been away down south for the Verdun show, has come back, and planted itself right opposite Wilks' crowd, and they don't think much of it.

'Wilks said it was about time the Boeleke crowd had their wings clipped, and I told him that the sooner he got on with the clipping the better—there was nothing to stop him going right ahead. He turned all nerky and asked why we didn't do something about it, and so on, and so forth.

'To cut a long story short, he suggested that I should do the decoy act for them. The idea was to rendezvous over Hamel at ten-thirty, me at twelve thousand feet up, and all the S.E. planes they could muster at eighteen thousand feet. I was to draw the German Albatrosses down, and our S.E.'s would come down on top of them.

'Wilks was particularly anxious to have a crack from up top at the new fellow who is leading the Albatrosses—they don't know his name. That was about ten o'clock, and I, like a fool, said "O.K.", and pushed off.

'Well, I got up to twelve thousand over Hamel, as arranged, and hung about until I saw nine S.E.'s high up, pushing into Hunland, where I followed them, keeping underneath, of course.

'I found the Boche circus all right, or, at least, they found me—put it that way! I don't know how many there were, but the sky was black with them. However, I thought I'd do the job properly, so I headed on towards them as if I was blind.

'The Huns didn't waste any time. No, sir! They came

176

buzzing down as if I was the only Britisher in the sky, and every one was full-out to get me first.

'It tickled me to death to think what a surprise-packet they'd got coming when old Wilks and his mob arrived. I looked up to see where Wilks' lot were, and was just in time to see them disappearing over the horizon.

'That stopped me laughing. At first I couldn't believe it, but there was no mistake. The S.E.'s just went drifting on until they were out of sight. And there was me, up Salt Creek without a paddle. I'd aimed to bring the German circus down, and I'd succeeded.

'Oh, yes, there was no doubt about that! There they were, coming down like a swarm of wasps that had been starved for a million years!

'There I was, and there was the circus! But having got 'em, I didn't know what to do with 'em, and that's a fact!'

'What did you do with them?' asked Batson eagerly. He had only recently joined the squadron.

'Nothing,' Biggles said. 'Nothing at all. Don't ask fool questions. I came home,' he went on, 'and I didn't waste any time on the way, I can assure you. I went back to Wilks' place. Don't ask me how I got there, because I don't know. I half rolled most of the way, I admit, but the main thing was I got there.

'And what do you think I found? No, it's no use guessing—I'll tell you. I found Wilks and his crowd playing bridge—playing bridge! Can you beat that?

'He looked surprised when I barged in, as well he might, and then had the cheek to say he thought I meant that the show was to be done tomorrow!'

'What about the S.E.'s you saw?' asked Mahoney.

'It wasn't them at all. It was Squadron No. 311, who are just out from England, going off on escort duty to

177

meet some "Fours" that had gone over on a bombing raid. They didn't know anything about me, of course, but when they got back they sent word to Wing Headquarters that they saw a Hun flying a Camel.

'They were sure it must have been a Hun, because they saw it fly straight up to the Boche formation. I was the poor boob they saw, and if that's their idea of joining a formation, I hope they never join one of ours.'

'But what did Wilks say about it?'

'He laughed—they all did—and said he was sorry. Then he had the nerve to suggest that I stayed to lunch. I told him that I hoped his lunch would give him corns on the gizzard, and then I pushed off back here.'

'What are you going to do about it?' asked Algy.

'I don't know yet,' replied Biggles slowly. 'But it'll be something, you can bet your life on that!'

For the next hour Biggles sat on the veranda, contemplating the distant horizon, and then a slow smile spread over his face. He rose to his feet and sought Algy, whom he found at the sheds, making some minor adjustments to his guns.

'Algy!' he called. 'Come here! I want you. I've got it.'

'Got what?'

'The answer. I'm going to pull old Wilks' leg so hard that he will never get it back into its socket, and I want your help.'

'Fine! Go ahead! What do I do?'

'First of all, I've got to get Wilks out of the way this afternoon for as long as possible; that is, I want to get him off the aerodrome. You know Wilks has a secret passion for those big lumps of toffee with stripes on.'

'Stripes on?'

178

'Yes, you know the things I mean—you get 'em at fairs and places.'

'You mean humbugs?'

'That's it—humbugs. Wilks has eaten every humbug for miles. What I want you to do is to ring up Wilks and tell him that you've discovered a new shop in Amiens where they have some beauties—enormous ones, pink, with purple stripes.

'Lay it on thick. Make his mouth water so much that he slobbers into the telephone. Tell him you've got a tender going to Amiens this very afternoon, and would he like to come?

'If he says yes, as I expect he will, tell him to fly over here right away, but he'd better not tell anyone where he is going, as you're not supposed to have the tender. I'll fix up the transport question with Tyler. You take Wilks to Amiens.

'If you can find a shop where they sell humbugs, well and good. If you can't you'll have to make some excuse—say you've forgotten the shop.

'Keep him out of the way as long as you can, and then bring him back here. He'll have to come back, anyway, to collect his machine.'

'And what are you going to do?'

'Never you mind,' replied Biggles. 'But, tell me, has Squadron No. 91 still got that Pfalz Scout* on their aerodrome—the one they forced to land the other day?'

'I think so; I saw it standing on the tarmac there a couple of days ago as I flew over.'

'Fine! That's all I want to know. You go and ring up Wilks and get him down to Amiens. Don't say anything about me. If he wants to know where I am, you can say I am in the air, which will be true.'

*Very successful German single-seater biplane fighter, fitted with two or three machine guns synchronised to fire through the propeller.

'Good enough, laddie!' said Algy. 'I'd like to know what the dickens you're going to get up to, but if you won't tell me, you won't. And that's that. See you later.'

# Chapter 21
# Returned Unknown

It was well on in the afternoon when a mechanic, who was snatching forty stolen winks on the shady side of the hangars on the aerodrome of Squadron No. 287, happened to open his eyes and look upwards. He started violently and looked again, and was instantly galvanised into life.

He sprang to his feet and sprinted like a professional runner towards a dugout by the gunpits, yelling shrilly as he went. His voice awoke the dozing aerodrome, and figures emerged from unexpected places.

Several officers appeared at the door of the mess, and after a quick glance upwards joined in the general rush, some making for the dugout and others for the revolving Lewis gun* that was mounted on an ancient cartwheel near the squadron office.

A medley of voices broke out, but above them a more urgent sound could be heard, the deep-throated song of a fast-moving aeroplane

The cause of the upheaval was not hard to discover. From out of a high thin layer of cloud had appeared an aeroplane of unmistakable German design; it was a Pfalz Scout. And it was soon apparent that its objective was Squadron No. 287's aerodrome.

Like a falling rocket the machine screamed earthwards. It flattened out some distance to the east of the

* Gun mounted on a scarf ring which completely encircled the gunner's cockpit allowing it to point in any direction. Also used on the ground, as here.

181

aerodrome, tore across the sheds at terrific speed, and then zoomed heavenward again, the pilot twisting his machine from side to side to avoid the bullets that he knew would follow him.

But his speed had been his salvation, for he was out of range before the gunners could bring their sights to bear.

As the machine disappeared once more into the cloud whence it had so unexpectedly appeared, two or three officers began running towards their machines. But, realising that pursuit was useless, they hurried towards the spot where a little crowd had collected.

'What is it?' cried one of them.

'Message,' was the laconic reply. 'I saw him drop it.'

The speaker tore the envelope from the streamer to which it was attached and ripped it open impatiently. His face paled as he read the note.

'It's Wilks,' he said in a low voice. 'He's down—over the other side!

'The Huns got him over Bettonau, half an hour ago—got his engine. By the courtesy of the C.O. of the Hun squadron where they have taken him, he has sent this message to say that he is unhurt, and would like someone to bring him over a change of clothes.

'He says he can have his shirts and pyjamas and pants—anything that we think might be useful. If someone will drop them on the Boche aerodrome at Douai, they will be handed to him before he is sent to the prison camp tonight.'

'I'll go!' cried several voices simultaneously.

Parker, a pilot of Wilks' flight, claimed the honour.

'Wilks was my pal,' he insisted, 'and this is the least I can do for him. I'll make a parcel of his small kit and all his shirts and things and drop them on the Hun aerodrome right away. Poor old Wilks!'

Sadly the speaker departed in the direction of Wilkinson's quarters, and half an hour later, watched by the sorrowful members of the squadron, the S.E. departed on its fateful journey.

Meantime, the pilot of the Pfalz Scout was not having a happy time. Twice he was sighted and pursued by British scouts, and although he managed to give them the slip, he was pestered continually by anti-aircraft gunfire, for his course lay, not over the German Lines, as one might have supposed, but behind the British Lines.

Finally, the black-crossed machine reached its objective, and started a long spin earthward, from which it did not emerge until it was very close to the ground in the immediate vicinity of Mont St. Eloi, the station of Naval Squadron No. 91.

The Pfalz made a couple of quick turns and then glided between the sheds of the aerodrome, afterwards taxi-ing quickly towards a little group of spectators.

The pilot—Biggles—switched off and climbed out of his cockpit, removing his cap and goggles as he did so. Lee, a junior officer in the Royal Naval Air Service uniform, broke from the group and hurried to meet him.

'What's the game, Bigglesworth?' he said shortly. 'You told me you only wanted to have a quick flip round the aerodrome. You've been gone more than half an hour.'

'Have I? Have I been away as long as that?' replied Biggles in well-simulated surprise. 'Sorry, old man, but I found the machine so nice to fly that I found it hard to tear myself out of the sky.'

'There'll be a row, you know, if it gets known that

you've been flying about over this side of the Line in a Hun machine. Besides, you must be off your rocker. I wonder our people didn't knock the stuffing out of you!'

'They did try,' admitted Biggles, 'but, really, I was most anxious to know just what a Pfalz could do. All our fellows ought to fly a Hun machine occasionally. It would help them to know how to attack it.'

'Perhaps you're right—but it would be thundering risky!'

'Yes, I suppose it would be,' admitted Biggles. 'But look here—in case there is a row, or if anyone starts asking questions about your Pfalz, I should be very much obliged if you'd forget that anyone has borrowed it. In any case, don't, for goodness' sake, mention my name in connection with it!'

'Right you are!' grinned Lee. 'Where are you off to now? Aren't you going to stay to tea?'

'No, thanks—I must get back. I've got one or two urgent things to attend to. Cheerio, laddie, and many thanks for the loan of your kite!'

With a parting wave, Biggles walked across to his Camel, took off, and set his nose in the direction of Maranique.

Biggles was comfortably seated in the ante-room, when, an hour later, a tender pulled up in front of the mess. Algy and Wilkinson, both apparently in high spirits, got out. Glancing in through the window, they saw Biggles inside, and entered noisily.

'What do you think about this poor boob?' began Wilks good-humouredly. 'He rang me up this afternoon to say that he was going to Amiens, and asked if I would like to come. He told me he knew of a shop where they sold the biggest humbugs in France, and then when we got to Amiens he couldn't remember where it was!'

'Yes, wasn't it funny?' agreed Algy. 'My memory is all going to blazes lately!'

'Yes, it's caused by castor oil soaking through the scalp into the brain!' declared Biggles. 'I've been like that myself. The best thing is to take a pint of petrol night and morning every day for a week, and then apply a lighted match to the tonsils.'

'Oh, shut up! Don't be a fool!' laughed Wilks. 'What about coming over to our place for dinner? We've got a bit of a show on tonight. We should have some fun.'

'That's O.K. by me!' declared Biggles.

'And me,' agreed Algy. 'What shall we do—go over by tender? We shan't be able to fly back, anyway; it'll be dark.'

'But I've got my kite here.'

'Never mind; leave it here until the morning—it'll take no harm.'

'Fine! Come on, then; let's go while the tender is still here.'

The S.E. pilots of Squadron No. 187 were at tea when, shortly afterwards, Biggles, Wilks and Algy entered the mess arm-in-arm. There was a sudden hush as they walked into the room. All eyes were fixed on Wilkinson.

'Hallo, chaps!' he called gaily. And then, observing the curious stares, he stopped dead and looked around him. 'What's wrong with you blighters?' he said. 'Have you all been struck with lockjaw?'

Parker, deadly white, crossed the room slowly and touched him gently on the chin with his finger.

'What's the idea?' Wilks said, in amazement. 'Think you're playing tag?' He turned to Biggles. 'Looks like we've come to a madhouse,' he observed.

'Is it you?' said Parker, in an awed whisper.

Wilks scratched his chin reflectively.

'I thought it was,' he said. 'It is me, Biggles, isn't it?'

'Absolutely you and nobody else,' declared Biggles.

'Come on, then, let's go through to my room and have a wash and brush up.'

Wilks led the way along the corridor and pushed open the door of his room, then staggered back with an exclamation of alarm.

'My hat!' he shouted. 'We've had burglars! Some skunk's pinched my kit!'

Biggles and Algy looked over his shoulder. The room was in terrific disorder. Drawers had been pulled out and their contents scattered over the floor. The lid of a uniform-case stood open, exposing an empty interior.

The room looked like the bedroom of an hotel that had been hurriedly evacuated. Wilks continued to stare at in incredulously.

'No,' said a small nervous voice behind them, 'it wasn't burglars—it was me.'

'You!' gasped Wilks. 'What do you mean by throwing my things all over the floor, you pie-faced rabbit? What have you done with my pyjamas, anyway? And where are my shirts, and—'

'I'm afraid your things are at Douai!'

'Douai!' Wilks staggered and sat down limply on the bed. 'Douai?' he repeated foolishly. 'What in the name of sweet glory would my clothes be doing at Douai? You're crazy!'

'I took them.'

Wilks swayed and his eyes opened wide.

'Do I understand you to say you've taken my clothes to Douai? Why Douai? Couldn't you think of anywhere else? I mean, if you wanted a joke you could have thrown them about the mess, or even out on the aerodrome! But Douai—I suppose you really mean Douai?'

'That's right.'

Wilks looked from Biggles to Algy and back again at Biggles.

'Can you hear what he says?' he choked. 'Did you hear him say that he'd taken my kit to—Douai?'

'When you were a prisoner,' explained Parker.

Wilks closed his eyes and shook his head savagely.

'I'm dreaming!' he muttered. 'You didn't by any chance see anybody dope that lemonade that I had in Amiens this afternoon, did you, Algy?'

'No,' replied Algy. 'I didn't, but I don't trust—'

'But a Hun dropped a message to say that you were a prisoner and wanted your kit!' explained Parker. 'Didn't he, chaps?' he called loudly to the officers who were now crowding into the corridor.

'But I haven't been near the Lines!' protested Wilks. 'Much less over them. Come here, Parker and tell me just what happened.'

As quickly and concisely as possible Parker narrated the events of the afternoon.

'The skunks!' grated Wilks. 'They must have got hold of my name somehow and planned some dirty trick. It's just like them. This business isn't finished yet—Hallo, what's that?' He sprang to his feet as the roar of an aero-engine vibrated through the air.

'That's no S.E.!' he muttered, staring at the others.

'By gosh, it isn't!' cried Biggles. 'It's a Mercedes engine, or I've never heard one. Look out, chaps, it's a Hun!' Without waiting for a reply, he darted towards the door. Sharp yells of alarm came from outside, and the staccato chatter of a machine-gun split the air.

For a minute or two pandemonium reigned as people rushed hither and thither, some for shelter and others

187

for weapons, but by the time they had reached them the danger had passed. A Pfalz Scout was disappearing into the distance, zig-zagging as if a demon was on its tail.

A hundred yards away a large, dark round object was bounding across the aerodrome. A mechanic started towards it, but Wilks shouted him back.

'Keep away from that, you fool!' he bellowed. 'Stand back, everybody!' he went on quickly, throwing himself flat. Biggles and Algy lay beside him and watched the object suspiciously.

'I'm taking no risks!' declared Wilks emphatically. 'I wouldn't trust a Hun an inch. It's some jiggery-pokery, I'll be bound. Keep down, everybody! That thing'll go bang in a minute, but I'll settle it!'

He jumped up and sprinted towards the nearest machine-gun, reaching it safely and, taking careful aim, sent a stream of tracer bullets through the small, balloon-like object.

It rolled over slowly, but did not explode. He fired another burst.

Again the object rolled over and jumped convulsively, but nothing else happened. A cheer broke from the spectators, in which Wilks joined.

'I'll make quite sure of it!' he cried, and emptied the remainder of a drum of ammunition into it. Rat-at-at-at-at—rata-rata-rata-rata! The object twitched and jerked as the hail of lead struck it.

'All right, I think it's safe now!' he went on, advancing slowly. Several of the watchers rose and followed him to where it lay, smoking at several jagged holes where the bullets had struck it. An aroma of singeing cloth floated across the aerodrome.

A low, strangled cry came from Parker, but no one noticed it.

'What the dickens is it?' muttered Wilks curiously. He stooped over the bundle and, with a sharp movement of his penknife, cut the cords that held it together.

It burst open, disclosing what appeared to be a number of old pieces of rag. Wilks picked up one of them and held it in the air. It was a piece of blue silk, punctured with a hundred holes, some of which were still smouldering.

'Why, it looks like a pyjama jacket, doesn't it?' he said, smiling. 'It would be a joke if we've shot some poor chap's pyjamas to rags. Yes, they're pyjamas all right,' he went on slowly, turning the rag round and round.

'By gosh, they're *my* pyjamas!' His voice rose to a bellow of rage. He flung the tattered debris of the garment on the ground and stamped on it.

'Wait a minute, here's a note!' shouted Parker. He picked up a mangled piece of paper and smoothed it out on his knee. 'It's in English, too! Listen! "From Jagdstaffel Commander, Douai. Message not understood. No Captain Wilkinson at Douai. Have made inquiries at other units, but no explanation received. Thinking mistake has been made, kit is returned with compliments." That is all!'

'But how did he know the clothes were for me?' demanded Wilks.

'Because I put a note in addressed to you,' replied Parker.

Wilks looked down at the mutilated remains of his underwear, and then started. His gaze ran over the assembled S.E.5 pilots, a new suspicion dawning in his eyes.

'By James, I've got it!' he exploded. 'Young Algy Lacey rang me up and asked me if I liked humbugs,' he went on quickly, 'and then he said he knew where there were some! He was right—he did! And so do I—now. Where is he, by the way, and that skunk Biggles?' He glanced around swiftly.

'They were here a moment ago,' ventured someone.

'I saw them hurrying towards the road,' said another.

There was a wild rush towards the main road that skirted the aerodrome. Far away a tender was racing down the long, white, poplar-lined highway, leaving a great cloud of dust in its wake.

# Chapter 22
# 'He Shot Him to Bits!'

Algy Lacey ran into the officers' mess of Squadron No. 266, R.F.C., and cast a swift, cautious glance around the room.

'Biggles is on the way here. He's in a blazing white-hot fury!' he said quickly. 'Let him get it off his chest—ahem!' He broke off and reached for the bell as Biggles, the subject of his warning, kicked the door open and glared at the speaker from the threshold.

Biggles' face was dead white; his lips were pressed into a thin, straight line; his nostrils quivered. His eyes, half-closed, glinted as they swept over the assembled officers.

'You're a nice lot of poor skates,' he observed, in a half-choked voice. 'It's time some of us got down to a little war, instead of playing fool games like a lot of kids!'

'All right—pour yourself out some tea, and get it off your chest,' suggested Maclaren calmly. He had seen the symptoms before.

Biggles glared at him belligerently. He seemed to have difficulty in finding his voice.

'Where's Wilson?' asked Mahoney.

'Wilson's dead!' replied Biggles shortly. Wilson was an officer who had recently transferred to Squadron No. 266 from a two-seater squadron.

'How did it happen?'

'I don't know. I saw him going down in flames, but I didn't know whether it was Wilson or Lacey until I

191

got back. Wilson was bound to get it sooner or later, the way he flew. He acted as if the sky was his own.'

'Well, don't let it worry you!' muttered Mahoney.

'That's not worrying me. It was only—'

Biggles broke off, buried his face in his hands, and was silent for some seconds. Nobody spoke. Mahoney caught Algy's eye, and grimaced. Algy shrugged his shoulders. Biggles drew a deep breath, and looked up.

'Sorry, blokes,' he said slowly, 'but I'm a bit het up! Any tea left in that pot?'

Mahoney pushed the teapot towards him.

'You remember young Parker, of Wilks' squadron?' went on Biggles.

'Yes. Nice lad! I always had an idea he'd do well. Got two or three Huns already, hasn't he?'

'He had,' replied Biggles. 'They don't count now. They got him—this afternoon—murdered him!'

'What are you talking about?' Mahoney said tersely.

Biggles made a sweeping gesture with his hand.

'Let me tell you,' he said. 'Listen here, chaps! I did the evening show today with Algy and Wilson. We worked round the Harnes, Annœulin, Don area. Just before we got to Annœulin I saw some S.E.'s ahead—four of 'em! Presently I saw it was Wilks and his Flight, so we linked up.

'There was nothing doing for a long time, and I thought it was going to be a wash-out, when a great mob of Huns suddenly blew along from the direction of Seclin. We ought not to have taken them on. There were too many of 'em—but that's by the way.

'They were a new lot to me—Albatross D.5's, orange with black stripes—it was a "circus" I've never seen before. Wilks turned towards them, and I followed, and then I don't quite know what happened.' Biggles paused and puckered his forehead.

'They were a pretty rotten lot, or none of us would have got back,' he went on. 'They flew badly, and shot all over the place. Two of 'em flew straight into each other. They struck me as being a new mob that had just come up from a flying school as a complete unit— except the three leaders, who, of course, would be old hands. They wore green streamers—at least, one of 'em did—the only one I saw. Did you notice anything, Algy?'

'I saw one with red streamers.'

'I didn't. No matter. Towards the finish, I saw Parker going down with a dead propellor—looked to me as if it had been shot off. Still, he was gliding comfortably enough, and was bound to land over the German side, when this Hun with the green streamers comes along, spots him, and goes down after him.

'There was no need for him to do it; Parker was going down a prisoner, anyhow. I'll give Parker full marks; he put up a jolly good show, although he couldn't do anything else but go down. He kept his eye on Green Streamers, and side-slipped from side to side so that he couldn't be hit.

'No man worth a hang would shoot a fellow who was helpless and bound to be taken prisoner whatever else happened. It isn't done. But Green Streamers— whether because he was sore because he couldn't hit him, or whether it was because he wanted a flamer to make his claim good, I don't know—shot at Parker all the way down. Even then he couldn't hit him, and Parker managed to make a landing of sorts in a stubble-field.

'I had to take my eyes off him then, because a couple more were at me, but I happened to look down again just as Parker was climbing out of his machine, waving to let us know he was all right. Green Streamers, the skunk, went right down at him, and—and—' Biggles' lips quivered, and the hand that held the teacup trembled.

'He shot him' he went on, after a short pause. 'Shot him to bits, in cold blood! I saw the tracer bullets kick up the ground around him. Parker just grabbed at his chest, then pitched forward on to his face. I went at Green Streamers like a bull at a gate, but some of the others got in my way, and I couldn't reach him. Then I lost him altogether, and didn't see him again.

'The Huns all made off, heading towards Seclin. I was so mad that I followed them to see where they lived, and, as I expected, they went down at Seclin, where the old Richthofen crowd used to be.

'I went down low on my way back, and saw Parker lying just as he had fallen, with a lot of German troops standing about. He was dead. There's no doubt of that, or they'd have moved him.'

'The pigs!' growled Mahoney. 'What does Wilks say about it?'

'I don't know. I haven't seen him to speak to. Huns have done the same thing once or twice before, and they always make the same excuse—say they thought the fellow was trying to set light to his machine. That doesn't go with me. Parker was, as I say, a prisoner, anyway. And I shouldn't shoot a Hun who was down over our side for trying to do what I should do myself, and—'

Biggles broke off as the door was flung open, and Wilkinson, followed by half a dozen pilots of his squadron, entered. They were still in their flying-suits, and had evidently come over by tender. Wilks' face was chalky white, and his eyes blazed. He came to a halt just inside the room, and pointed at Biggles.

194

'You saw it, didn't you, Biggles?' he snapped in a tense voice.

Biggles nodded.

'There you are, chaps!' went on Wilks, over his shoulder. He turned to Biggles again and jerked his thumb behind him. 'They wouldn't believe me—said not even a Hun would do a thing like that!'

'Well, what about it?' asked Maclaren.

Wilks flung his cap across the room viciously.

'This!' he said bitterly. 'I'm going to get that Hun with the green decorations on his struts! If someone else happens to be flying that machine, it will be his unlucky day!'

'Never mind Green Streamers,' put in Biggles. 'I'll bet he's told the rest of his crowd about it by this time, and they'll be laughing like hyenas. I say, let us mop up the whole lot of 'em, good and proper! We can't have people like this about the place!'

'Good idea! But how?' asked Mahoney.

Biggles thought deeply for a moment.

'I'll tell you,' he replied. 'Sit down, you chaps,' he added to the newcomers. 'There was a time when people over here who flew behaved like gentlemen. But there has lately been a tendency towards the methods of the original Huns, and I say it is up to us to put the blighters where they belong.

'Let us keep our department of this confounded war clean, or life won't be worth living.

'For a start, we'll deal with this orange-and-black lot of tigers. But don't forget this—it's no use our going on as we have been working. If we do, our patrols will meet this crowd and get the worst of it. They've taken to flying together, while we go on flying in bits and pieces, in twos and threes. That's no use—it won't get us anywhere.

195

'If everyone is willing, let us get together and make a clean job of it. I should say there are thirty machines in that new Hun group—three "staffels". It's no earthly use three of us taking on that crowd, but if we put up all our machines together—say two complete squadrons, eighteen machines or thereabouts—it will be a different proposition.'

'What's the debate?'

Major Mullen, the C.O., with Major Benson, of Squadron No. 301 entered the mess and looked around curiously.

Briefly, Biggles told him of the affair of the afternoon, and the drastic steps he was going to suggest to him in order to make their displeasure known to the orange staffels.

'But if you start cruising about, eighteen strong, you don't suppose you will ever get near the Huns, do you?' asked Major Mullen. 'Small patrols are their meat.'

'I've thought of that, sir,' replied Biggles. 'We shall have to use cunning, that's all. The Hun hasn't much imagination, but he is a very methodical bloke, and it is on that score that I propose to get him going. Tomorrow morning, at the crack of dawn, I shall go over and shoot up Seclin.'

'Alone?'

'If necessary, or with two other officers, if they'll come. I don't want anybody detailed for the job; I'd ask for volunteers.'

'I'll come,' put in Algy quickly, and Mahoney put up his hand.

Several other officers stepped forward.

'That's enough,' declared Biggles. 'You can't all come. Now, this is my idea. Tomorrow morning three of us will shoot the spots off Seclin aerodrome. The next morning, at exactly the same time, we'll do it

196

again. After the second show, it will occur to the Hun that these dawn shows are going to be a regular institution, and they'll decide to do something about it.

'On the third morning we shall go over as usual, and the Hun, unless I am very much mistaken, will be up top-sides bright and early, waiting for us. As it happens, we shall not be alone. The three machines will fly low, as usual, but six more Camels will be at, say, six thousand.

'The Huns may see them; in fact, I hope they do, because they'll think it is the escort, and not bother to look any further. They won't see nine S.E.'s up at twelve thousand, waiting for the show to begin before they come down. They won't hear them because they'll be in the air, and the noise of their own engines will settle that.

'So, when the show begins, there will be eighteen of us on the spot, and the Hun will find he is up to the neck in the gravy. That is how I hope we shall wipe these blighters and their perishing aerodrome off the map. Anybody else got any ideas?'

There was no response to the question.

'That's fine, then,' went on Biggles. 'One last thing, though. If we succeed in pushing these blighters into the ground—and we certainly shall—I suggest that we all go back straight away and strafe their sheds. That will be the finishing touch—make a clean job of it, so to speak.'

The C.O. thought for a moment.

'I've no objection,' he said. 'As a matter of fact, we shall probably profit by it in the end, because if we don't do something of the sort the Huns, by working together, will be certain to cause casualties amongst the small patrols and individual pilots.'

'Grand! I feel better now,' declared Biggles. 'We'll

get out times and rendezvous later on. We'll start the action tomorrow, Tuesday, which means that this big show will be on Thursday. Now I'm going to have a bath.

It was still quite dark when Biggles' batman* called him the following morning. Biggles sat up in bed, gulped down the proffered tea, and shivered.

'Have you called Captain Mahoney and Mr Lacey?' he inquired.

'Yes, sir; they're both dressing.'

Biggles crawled out of bed as the batman withdrew.

'The number of times I've said that I'd never volunteer for any more of these cock-crow shows—and here I am at it again,' he grumbled. 'Grrrr.'

He pulled his sheepskin thigh-boots on over his pyjamas, donned a thick, high-necked woollen sweater, and then his leather flying-coat. He adjusted his flying-helmet, leaving the chin-strap flapping, and slipped his goggles over it. Then he walked through to the mess to drink another cup of tea and munch a biscuit while he waited for the others.

Mahoney and Algy followed him into the mess almost immediately, and in reply to his terse: 'If you're ready, we'll get off,' followed him to the sheds, whence came the roar of engines being run up.

All was still on the aerodrome. A faint flush was stealing across the eastern sky, and the stars began to lose their brightness.

'You lead,' said Biggles, looking at Mahoney. 'If I were you, I should go straight over, keeping low all the way. When we get there, do three circles to the left, and then hit the breeze for home, rallying on the way.

* An attendant serving an officer. A position discontinued in today's RAF.

We'll pull our bomb-toggles* for four bombs first time, four the second time, and use our guns the third time. How's that?'

'Sounds all right to me,' said Mahoney. 'Come on!'

The three pilots climbed into their seats, ran up their engines to confirm that they were giving their full revs, waved away the chocks, and then took off straight across the aerodrome without troubling to taxi out, for there was not a breath of wind.

Keeping low, they raced across the British trenches at a hundred feet, startling the troops, and made a beeline for their objective. It took them exactly ten minutes to reach it, after crossing the lines. As it came into sight, Mahoney, in the lead, edged a little to the right, and then tore straight at the line of camouflaged canvas hangars.

The aerodrome was deserted. Not a soul or an aeroplane was to be seen. The only sign of life was a small party of crows just in front of the German sheds.

Biggles followed Mahoney in his downward rush at an interval of perhaps twenty yards. Algy brought up the rear. As Biggles reached for the bomb toggle he saw several people, obviously in night attire, run out of the huts that stood just behind the hangars and throw themselves flat. He waited until the first hangar came in line with the junction of his starboard wing and fuselage, and then pulled.

He saw Mahoney's bombs burst in quick succession as he zoomed upwards, taking a nasty bump from his leader's slip-stream as he did so. Banking left, and glancing back over his shoulder, he saw figures running. A great cloud of smoke concealed the buildings,

* The bomb release handles.

so it was impossible to see what damage had been done.

A long stream of tracer bullets leapt upwards from a point near the edge of the aerodrome, but Biggles only smiled. Still keeping in line, the three Camels swung round into their previous tracks and swooped low over the drifting smokecloud. Mahoney's four remaining bombs swung off the racks, and his own followed. He turned left again as the last one left his machine. This time he did not go entirely unscathed, for several bullet holes had appeared in his wings. He smiled again, and settled himself low in the cockpit for the final plunge.

All three Camels had zoomed to a thousand feet over the edge of the aerodrome, and now, as one machine, they banked steeply again and screamed down on the Boche sheds. Biggles could see Mahoney's tracer bullets pouring into the smoke, for the target was no longer visible, and his hand groped for the gun lever.

A double stream of tracer bullets poured from the muzzles of his guns. He held the burst until his wheels were actually in the smoke, and then soared up in a climbing turn.

Algy roared up beside him, goggles pushed up, laughing. Mahoney was some distance ahead, but he throttled back to enable them to catch up, and in a tight arrow-head formation they made for home.

The return trip was an uneventful journey, although they came in for a good deal of attention from troops on the ground, as was only to be expected. Mahoney left the formation for a few moments to chase a staff car, returning after the panic-stricken driver had turned the vehicle over at the first bend. They reached Maranique just before six, having been in the air for under an hour.

'How did it go?' called Wat Tyler from the squadron office as they passed it on the way down to breakfast.

'Fine!' replied Biggles. 'We just left our cards and came home!'

'How did it go?' asked Wat Tyler from the squadron
office as they passed on their way down to breakfast.

'Ow!' replied Biggles. 'We just left our cards and
came home.'

# Chapter 23
# 'Written Off'

On Thursday morning, at a quarter to five, Major
Mullen addressed eight other pilots in front of A. Flight
shed. A short distance away, nine Camels stood in
readiness for the impending 'show'.

'I'll just run over everything once more, so that there
can be no possibility of mistake. As you. all know,
one flight has already made two raids on the German
aerodrome at Seclin. The second raid, made yesterday
morning, was carried out at exactly the same time and
in the same way as the first one.

'Yesterday the enemy were ready—or perhaps it
would be more correct to say nearly ready. They had
their machines lined up on the tarmac, but were unable
to get off in time to catch ours. It is hoped that they
will actually be in the air this morning, awaiting a
recurrence of the attack.

'Mahoney, Bigglesworth and Lacey will fly low and
raid the aerodrome as usual—at least, they will behave
as if they are going to. Whether they do it or not
depends upon circumstances. It is the riskiest part of
the show, but they insist on doing it, and as they are
best qualified for the job, knowing the lay-out of the
aerodrome intimately, I have agreed.

'I shall lead the remaining six Camels at six thousand
feet. If the Huns are not in the air, we shall remain
where we are, acting as escort to the lower formation.
If, however, the Huns are in the air, they will attack
the lower formation first, and we shall go to their assist-

202

ance. The S.E.'s, which will be flying above us, will immediately join issue.

'I want every officer to stand by and do his level best to destroy at least one enemy machine.

'You all know the reason of this attack, so I need not go into it again. Our ultimate object is the complete write-off of this particular German group. A red light will be my signal to rally. That's all. Start up!'

Biggles threw his half-smoked cigarette aside and climbed into his seat. A savage exultation surged through him, for the next half-hour would see the culmination of his plan. Whether it would result in failure or success remained to be seen. The urge to fight was on him. More than anything else he wanted to see the machine with the green streamers!

The sudden bellow of an engine warned him that his leader was taking off. He waved away his chocks, and the three Camels roared into the still air. They circled the aerodrome once to allow the other six machines to gain altitude, and then swung east on the course they had followed the two previous mornings.

They escaped the usual front line archie, for it concentrated on the higher machines, which offered an easier target, but they came in for a certain amount of trouble from rifles and machine-guns on the ground.

Biggles took a final glance round to see that all was in order. Twenty yards to the right he could see Algy's muffled profile, and, to the front, the back of Mahoney's head. Looking backwards and upwards over his shoulder, he could see the other six Camels following on, but of the S.E.5's there was no sign, due, possibly, to the slight haze that still hung in the sky.

The objective aerodrome loomed up in the near distance, and Biggles, leaning far out of his cockpit, stared long and earnestly upwards. He closed his eyes for a moment, pushed up his goggles, and looked again, and a muttered exclamation broke from his lips as he saw what he had hoped to see—the entire German circus!

His plan for getting them into the air had worked, but a sudden feeling of anxiety assailed him as he counted their numbers. He made it twenty-nine the first time and twenty-eight the second. They were flying on a westerly course, and changed direction as he watched them.

'They've spotted us,' he muttered.

Mahoney shook his wings, and Biggles smiled.

'All right, old son—I can see 'em,' he murmured. 'Here they come!'

The Huns were coming—there was no doubt of that—and to an inexperienced pilot the sight would have been an unnerving one. Like a cloud of locusts they poured through the sky, plunging downwards in a ragged formation towards the approaching Camels.

'Well, I hope those perishing S.E.'s are on time!' was Biggles' last thought as he swung out a little to allow Mahoney and Algy to manœuvre without risk of collision. 'What a mob! This looks like being a show and a-half! I shouldn't be surprised if somebody gets hurt!'

If the Huns felt any surprise that the three Camels should continue on their way in spite of the inspiring reception prepared for them, they did not show it. Straight down, at a terrific angle they roared; in fact, so steeply did they dive that Biggles felt a thrill of apprehension lest they should ram them before they could pull out.

He stared at the Hun leader to see if he was wearing streamers, but from the angle at which he was approaching it was impossible to see if his wing struts carried them or not. Where were the rest of the Camels and the S.E. 5's? Good! There were the Camels cutting across at terrific speed to intercept the Huns, but there was no sign of the S.E.'s. If they were late, even although it was only two minutes—

Biggles thrust the thought aside, put down his nose a trifle for speed, and then zoomed up to meet the attack. It was no use trying to keep in formation now.

The first casualty occurred before a shot had been fired. A Camel pilot of the top layer, seeing that he was in danger of colliding with a Hun, swerved to avoid him, and struck another that he had evidently not seen square in the side of the fuselage. Both machines disintegrated in a mighty cloud of flying debris.

A second Hun who was close behind swerved wildly to avoid them, but failed to do so. His wing struck the remains of his comrade's machine; it broke in halves near the centre section, and he too, plunged earthwards. Three machines—two Huns and a Camel— were hurtling down to oblivion before the fight commenced.

As the first two collided, Biggles shuddered involuntarily; he could almost sense the shock of the impact. But there was no time for contemplation.

From such a cloud of machines it was hard to single one out for individual attack, but he saw an Albatross firing at him, and accepted the challenge. For a full minute they spun dizzily round each other, neither gaining an advantage, and then the Hun burst into flames.

Biggles was not shooting at the time, nor did he see the machine from which the shots had come to send the Boche to his doom. He turned sharply to the right and caught his breath, for it almost looked as if fighting was out of the question. The air was stiff with machines, diving, half rolling, and whirling around in indescribable confusion. It would need all the pilots' wits to avoid collision, much less take aim.

Another Hun was in flames, but still under control, with the pilot on his lower plane side-slipping downwards.

It seemed to Biggles that no one could hope to escape collision in such hopeless chaos. Machines of both sides hurtled past him at frenzied speed, sometimes missing him by inches. It was dodge and dodge again. Shooting was of the wildest snapshot variety.

Then, suddenly, the air seemed to clear, as if there were less machines than there had been. A Camel tore across his nose with an orange-and-black Hun on its tail. Biggles made a lightning turn to follow, saw the Camel burst into flames, fired, and saw the Hun pilot sag forward in the cockpit. An orange wing spun upwards, and the torpedo-shaped fuselage dropped like a bomb.

A burst of bullets struck Biggles' machine somewhere just behind him, and he jerked the control-stick back into his stomach. A Hun shot past his wing-tip, so close that Biggles flinched.

'That's too close!' he muttered. 'Where the dickens are the S.E.'s?'

He could see some of the Albatrosses turning away, as if they had had enough, and then out of the blue a cloud of brightly coloured Fokker triplanes tore into the fight. The fleeing Albatrosses turned again and headed back to the fight.

Biggles stared.

'My hat!' he ejaculated. 'It's the Richthofen crowd— and the blinking baron himself!' he added, as his eyes fell on a blood-red triplane.

His mouth set grimly and he twisted to bring his sights to bear, but was forced to turn away as an orange

Albatross shot across his path. It was followed by another with green streamers fluttering from its V-shaped interplane struts. He jerked his machine round spasmodically to follow, and saw that an S.E. was already pursuing it. It was Wilkinson's.

'Out of my way, Wilks!' yelled Biggles, completely carried away.

He saw the S.E. slip sideways to escape a burst of fire directed at it by the red triplane, and it left the way clear. He crouched forward, peering through his gun-sights, saw the green streamers, and fired. The Albatross turned over and spun.

'No, you don't!' snarled Biggles. 'You can't get away with that!'

His suspicion that the Hun was shamming was well founded, for after two or three spins the Boche recovered control and dived away.

But Biggles had followed him down. The Hun made a bad turn that almost caused him to stall, and for a couple of seconds Biggles had a 'sitter'. Taca-taca-taca-taca! sang his guns.

The Hun turned slowly over on to its back, and, with the tell-tale streamers still fluttering in the slipstream, roared earthwards, black smoke pouring from its engine.

Biggles suddenly remembered the Richthofen circus. 'This looks like being a bad business,' he thought. 'The Huns outnumber us now by at least two to one.'

He looked up, and a yell broke from his lips. A Bristol Fighter, with its gunner crouched like a monkey behind the rear gun, cut clean through the dog-fight. Another and another followed it—the air was full of Bristols.

'Gosh! It's Benson and his crowd! He heard us discussing it, and decided to butt in at the death,' was the thought that flashed through his mind.

Then he started and stared incredulously as an R.E.8 swam into view, heading for the thickest of the fighting, and three D.H.4's suddenly appeared on the right.

'What the dickens is happening?' he muttered. 'If this goes on much longer the whole blinking Flying Corps will be here!'

It was almost true. Machines of all types, two-seaters and scouts, seeing the fight from afar, decided to take a hand, but it was unquestionably the arrival of the Bristol Fighters at the crucial moment that saved the day. Shortly after their arrival there must have been at least a hundred machines engaged, and the Huns began to disappear like magic. Presently all the machines that Biggles could see were British; the Huns had had enough.

Turning slowly, he looked around and saw a red Very light flare sinking earthward; it was Major Mullen's signal to rally. Looking up, Biggles saw him circling above, and climbed up to join him. The major did not wait, but set off towards the lines, several Camels following in loose order.

Biggles landed and joined the C.O. on the tarmac.

'Did you ever see anything like that in your life, sir?' he cried as he ran up. If anybody ever asks me if I've been in a dog-fight I shall now be able to say "Yes"!'

Within ten minutes several Camels had landed, and he knew there would be no more.

'What about this bombing trip?' he asked the C.O.

'Yes, we're going to do it,' replied the major. 'All three squadrons are going to rendezvous over the aerodrome in half an hour. Get filled up as fast as you can, everybody—petrol and ammunition.'

Thirty minutes later a mixed formation of Camels,

S.E.5's and Bristol Fighters headed once more toward the scene of the great air battle.

The formation reached the aerodrome without opposition, and, diving low, laid their eggs. The Seclin aerodrome became a blazing inferno, although just how frightful was the damage inflicted was not revealed until a reconnaissance machine returned with photographs the following morning. Seclin aerodrome had been written off, as Biggles had planned!

'Well, that's a bonnie picture!' observed Biggles next morning as he examined the photograph of the stricken aerodrome. 'We said we'd wipe 'em out, and, by gosh, we have. Wilks agrees that we have settled Parker's account for him!'

# Chapter 24
# Under Open Arrest!

Algy Lacey, of No. 266 squadron had no intention of landing at Cassel when he took off on a short test flight. But after wandering aimlessly through the blue for some minutes and finding himself within easy distance of the aerodrome he decided he would drop in and leave his card at the mess of the new squadron—No. 301—that had recently arrived in France from England with its Bristol Fighters.

In accordance with the custom at the time, he did not land immediately. For the honour and glory of the squadron to which he belonged he first treated any casual spectators of his arrival to a short performance in the art of stunting.

He pushed his nose down and roared low over the mess—so low that his wheels almost touched the roof, in order to indicate his show was about to commence.

Thereafter, at various altitudes he proceeded to put his machine through every evolution known to aviation. Loops, slow rolls, fast rolls, barrel rolls, half rolls, rolls on top of loops, whip stalls and Immelmann* turns followed each other in quick succession, until feeling slightly giddy, he decided he had done enough.

He cut out his engine, glided in between the hangars in a manner that effectually scattered his audience,

---

* An Immelmann turn consists of a half roll off the top of a loop, thereby reversing the direction of flight. Named after Max Immelmann, German fighter pilot 1914–1916 with seventeen victories, who was the first to use this turn in combat.

then skidded round to a neat one-wheeled, cross-wind landing. Satisfied that he had upheld the traditions of No. 266 Squadron, he then taxied, tail-up, towards the sheds.

Only when collision with the line of machines at the end of the tarmac seemed inevitable did he swing round and come to a stop, a bare ten yards from the re-assembled spectators.

Whistling happily, he leapt lightly to the ground, took off his cap and goggles, threw them into his seat, and, with a broad smile on his face, advanced towards the members of the new squadron.

One stood a little apart from the others, and at the expression on his face Algy's lost something of its gaiety and acquired a new look of faint surprise.

The isolated officer, whom Algy now observed wore on his arm the three stars of a captain, took a pace towards him.

'Who are you?' he barked, in such a peremptory voice that Algy jumped.

The greeting was unusual, to say the least of it.

'Why—er—I'm Lacey, of No. 266,' replied Algy, startled.

'Say "sir" when you speak to me! I am in command here during the temporary absence of Major Benson!'

'Sorry, sir!' replied Algy, abashed and not a little astonished.

'What do you mean by acting like a madman over my aerodrome?' the other demanded.

Algy blinked and looked helplessly at the other officers. 'Not like a madman, sir, I hope!'

'Don't argue with me! I say your flying was outrage-ous—a wanton risk of Government property!'

'But I—'

'Silence! Consider yourself under open arrest! Report

211

your name and unit to my office, and then return instantly to your own squadron! I shall refer the matter to Wing Headquarters. You will hear further from your own C.O.'

Algy stiffened and swallowed hard.

'Very good, sir!' he ground out between his clenched teeth.

He saluted briskly, reported to the squadron office as instructed, then returned to the tarmac.

Several officers regarded him sympathetically. One of them winked and inclined his head.

Algy halted near him.

'What's the name of that dismal Jonah?' he said softly. 'And what's biting him, anyway? Has he had a shock of some sort, or is it just plain nasty-mindedness?'

'That's it—born like it! They must have fed him on crab apples when he was a kid. Watch out, though—he's acting C.O.'

'What's his name?'

'Bitmore.'

'He's bit more than he can chew this time, and he'll soon know it!' declared Algy. 'Has he been to France before?'

'No.'

'Then how did he get those three pips on his sleeve?'

'Chasing poor little pupils round the tarmac at a flying training school.'

'Well, this isn't one, and he isn't chasing me!' snapped Algy. 'My crowd will soon show him where he steps out if he's going to try being funny! The sooner some nice friendly Hun pushes him into the ground the better for everybody. Give your blokes my condolences. Cheerio!'

'Cheerio, laddie!'

Algy climbed into his machine, took off, and raced

back to Maranique. He parked his Camel in its usual place in front of the sheds and marched stiffly towards the squadron office. On the way he met a party of officers, including Biggles and Mahoney, on their way to the hangars.

'Stand aside!' he said curtly as they moved to intercept him. 'I'm under arrest.'

Biggles stopped dead.

'You're what?' he gasped.

'Under arrest.'

'Arrest my foot! What's the game?'

'No game—it's a fact. I went to call on No. 301 Squadron this morning—you know, the new crowd over at Cassel—and I gave them the once-over before I landed. When I got down a mangy skunk named Bitmore, who is acting C.O., dressed me down properly and put me under open arrest.'

'Your show must have given him a rush of blood to the brain.'

'Looks like it. Anyway, he's reporting me to Wing.'

Biggles frowned and looked at Mahoney.

'The dirty scallywag!' he muttered. 'What are we going to do about it? We can't have blighters like this about the place. Life won't be worth living. Think of what the poor chaps in his own squadron must go through. Quite apart from ourselves, I think we ought to do something for them. If Mr Bitmore is going to start chucking his weight about, it's time we did a bit of heaving ourselves!'

'Absolutely!' declared Mahoney.

'I tell you what,' went on Biggles, and, drawing Mahoney to one side, he whispered in his ear. Then he turned again to Algy.

'All right, laddie,' he said, 'you had better go and

213

report to Wat Tyler. You've had orders, and if you don't obey them it'll only make things worse.'

Algy departed in the direction of the squadron office, while Biggles and Mahoney walked quickly back towards their quarters.

A couple of hours later two Sopwith Camels appeared over the boundary of Squadron No. 301's aerodrome at Cassel. To the officers lounging on the tarmac and in front of the officers' mess it was at once apparent that neither of the pilots was adept in the art of flying.

Twice they circled the aerodrome, making flat turns and committing every other fault that turns the hair of instructors prematurely grey. Twice they attempted to land. The first time they undershot, and, opening up their engines at the last moment, staggered across the front of the sheds, scattering the watchers far and wide and narrowly missing disaster.

The second time they overshot hopelessly, and, skimming the trees on the far side of the aerodrome, skidded round to land down-wind. The spectators wiped the perspiration from their faces and groaned in unison, while the ambulance raced madly round, trying to anticipate the exact spot on which the crash would occur.

The first of the two machines made its third attempt to get in, and a cry of horror arose as the Camel drifted along on a course in a dead line with the wind-stocking pole.

At the last moment the pilot appeared to see it, skidded violently, missed it by an inch, and flopped down to a landing that would have disgraced a first-soloist. The second machine followed, grazing the mess roof, and together they taxied an erratic course up to the hangars.

The two pilots, clad in brand-new bright yellow flying coats and crash-helmets, climbed out of their machines and approached the little crowd of officers and air mechanics who had collected to watch the fun.

Slightly in front of them, Captain Bitmore stood waiting. He was in his element. Such moments were food and drink to his warped mentality. His taciturn face twisted itself into an expression in which disgust and rage were predominant.

'Come here!' he snarled.

Obediently the two officers altered their course towards him.

'What do you call yourselves?' went on Bitmore, curling his lip into a sneer. 'Pilots! Pilots, eh?' He choked for a moment, and then got into his stride with a harsh, scornful laugh. 'You're not fit to pilot a perambulator down a promenade, either of you!

'You're a disgrace to the Service! A steamroller driver could have put up a better show! Never have I seen such a disgraceful exhibition of utter inefficiency, complete uselessness, and supreme inability! How and why you are still alive is a mystery to me, and the sooner you are put on ground duties the safer the air will be for other people who *can* fly! You make me—'

His voice trailed away to silence that could be felt as the nearer of the two recipients of his invective slowly unfastened his flying-coat and took it off, disclosing the insignia of a full colonel. The other had followed his example, and stood arrayed in the uniform of a staff major.

The colonel eyed the captain with bold fury.

'Have you quite finished?' he said, in a voice that made the spectators shiver. 'Because, if you have, I will begin. What is your name?'

'Bitmore, sir.'

'Bitmore? Ah, I might have known it. I've heard of you for a useless, incompetent, incapable piece of inefficiency! Who is in command at this station?'

There was a titter from the other officers, but it faded swiftly as the colonel's eye flashed on them.

'I am, sir. I—'

'Silence! You dare to tell me that you are in command of a squadron, and take it upon yourself to criticise my flying! How long have you been in France?'

'Well, sir—'

'Don't "well" me—answer my question!'

'Two days, sir.'

'Aha! Two days, eh? No doubt you think that qualifies you to call yourself a war pilot—to question the actions of officers who have learnt their flying in the field. You dolt! You imbecile! You—'

He choked for breath for a moment, and then continued:

'I called here for petrol, and this is the reception I get!'

'I'm sorry, sir!'

'You will be, I promise you! Get my tanks filled up, and have your mechanics clean both machines. Come along—jump to it! We've no time to waste!'

Captain Bitmore, ashen-faced, lost no time in obeying the order, and the mechanics needed no urging. With smiles that they could not repress, the air mechanics set about the machines, and in ten minutes the two Camels were refuelled. Their props, wings and struts were polished until they looked as if they had only just left the workshops of the makers, but not until they were completely satisfied did the colonel and his aide-de-camp climb into their seats.

'I shall bear your name in mind,' was the colonel's

216

parting shot at the discomfited captain, as, with the major in attendance, he taxied out and took off.

A quarter of an hour later both machines landed at Maranique. The two pilots leapt to the ground, and, to the great surprise of Flight-Sergeant Smyth, they ran quickly round to the back of the hangars and then on to the officers' quarters. It struck Smyth, from their actions as they ran, that they were both in pain.

They were; but not until they were in Biggles' room and had discarded their borrowed raiment did the so-called staff officers give way to their feelings. Biggles lay on his bed and sobbed helplessly. Mahoney, with the major's jacket on the floor at his feet, buried his face in his hands and moaned weakly.

'Poor chap!' said Biggles at last, wiping his face with a towel. 'He'll never be able to live that down as long as he lives! Right in front of the whole blinking squadron, too! Still, it served him right.'

'My word, if he ever finds out there will be a rare old stink!' declared Mahoney.

But nothing happened, and by the next evening the incident was half forgotten.

# Chapter 25
# The Laugh's with Us!

Two days later a middle-aged officer, with an imposing array of medal ribbons on his breast, landed at Maranique and walked briskly towards the squadron office.

Major Mullen, the commanding officer of Squadron No. 266, was working at his desk, and looked up in surprise as the visitor entered. Then his face broke into a smile of welcome, and he sprang to his feet.

'Why, hallo, Benson!' he cried. 'I'm glad to see you again! What brings you here?'

Major Benson shook his hands warmly.

'I'm back over here again now,' he said. 'Just brought out a new squadron—No. 301. We're at Cassel, just over the way, so I hope we shall be seeing something of each other. I've been on a few days' leave, and sent the squadron ahead of me in charge of Bitmore, my senior flight-commander. I only got back this morning. I've brought a fine lot of chaps over, so I hope we shall do well.'

'Good—I hope you will!'

'But that isn't really why I came to see you. My people had an unexpected visit from two Wing officers the other day—awful nuisance, these people. I happened to run into Logan last night. You remember Logan, of General Headquarters? Well, he happened to mention that they were making a surprise inspection of your station some time today, so I thought I'd give you the tip.'

Major Mullen sprang to his feet.

'The dickens they are!' he cried. 'Thanks very much, Benson! Dash them and their surprise visits! They think we have nothing else to do but sit and polish our machines all day and sweep up the aerodrome. If everything isn't as clean as a new pin, this squadron gets a black mark. It isn't the number of Huns one gets in the war,' he added bitterly. 'G.H.Q. knows nothing about that!'

Major Benson nodded sympathetically.

'Don't I know it!' he said, 'Well I shall have to be getting back. No, I can't stay to lunch. I've a lot to do. Thanks all the same!'

'I shall have to get busy myself to get things in order for this inspection,' replied Major Mullen. 'Good-bye, Benson, and thanks awfully for giving me the tip! I hope we shall be seeing you again soon. I should like your fellows to get on well with mine.'

He lost no time in setting preparations on foot for the impending inspection. Telephones rang, N.C.O.'s chased mechanics to various tasks, and all officers were ordered out of the mess to help clean their machines.

For two hours the aerodrome presented a scene of unparalleled activity, and by the end of that time everything was in apple-pie order. All ranks were then dismissed to their quarters, with orders to parade in twenty minutes properly dressed, and in their best uniforms.

Biggles complained bitterly as he struggled with the fastenings of his collar.

'Confound all brass-hats!' he snarled. 'If I had my way—'

'All right! All right!' growled Algy. 'Don't keep on about it! It only makes it worse.'

With tightly laced boots, and well-brushed uniforms, they took their places on the tarmac.

'Everyone will stand by until further orders!' called the C.O.

The officers took their places by the respective machines. The minutes rolled by. An hour passed slowly, and nothing happened. Two hours passed, and still there was no sign of the staff officers—otherwise 'brass-hats'.

Biggles began to sag at the knees.

'My hat!' he groaned. 'I can't stand much more of this! Aren't we getting any lunch today, Mahoney?'

'The Old Man says no. The brass-hats might arrive at any moment, so we're to carry on until they come.'

Slowly the afternoon wore on, but still there was no sign of the expected officers. Then, from a distance, came the drone of many aeroplanes flying in formation, and the personnel of Squadron No. 266 stiffened expectantly.

'My word, they're doing the job properly!' muttered Algy to Biggles.

'Don't be a fool! Brass-hats don't fly!' snapped Biggles. 'Look! What's this coming? What the—'

He broke off, staring unbelievingly towards the far edge of the aerodrome as nine Bristol Fighters, flying very low in a beautiful tight Vee formation, swept into sight.

Straight across the aerodrome they roared. When they were about half-way, and immediately in front of the sheds, they dipped in ironical salute.

A message streamer fluttered to the ground from the leading machine. Then they disappeared from sight beyond the hangars, and the drone of their engines was lost in the distance.

An air-mechanic raced out, picked up the message, and carried it to the puzzled C.O.

Under the curious eyes of the entire squadron he

opened it. There was an extraordinary expression on his face as he looked up and called:

'Captain Mahoney and Captain Bigglesworth, please come here! What do you make of that?' he went on curtly as he passed a sheet of paper.

They read it together:

'It is requested that Captains Mahoney and Bigglesworth be asked how they like their eggs boiled.

'For and on behalf of the officers of Squadron No. 301.

'(Signed) A. L. BENSON, Major.'

'What a put-over!' gasped Biggles, as understanding flashed to him.

'Come with me!' said the C.O. curtly, and led the way to the squadron office. 'Now, gentlemen,' he went on as he closed the door behind them, 'kindly have the goodness to explain what all this is about.'

Biggles acted as spokesman. Clearly and concisely he told the whole story, from Algy's reprimand by Captain Bitmore up to the masquerade, and the admonition of that officer.

The major heard him out in silence.

'Well,' he said slowly, 'there are two aspects in this situation. Major Benson has evidently discovered the plot, and he has taken the course that I, knowing him as an officer of the finest type, would expect.

'If he had reported the matter officially to Headquarters I need hardly tell you that you would both have been court-martialled. As it is, he has taken an unofficial course to enable the squadron to get its own back. He has put it across us very neatly!

'At this moment every member of Squadron No. 301 is probably convulsed with mirth at our expense. We

221

shall never hear the last of it. The joke has recoiled on us with a vengeance. What are we going—'

The door was flung open, and Wat Tyler, the recording officer, dashed in.

'Staff car just arrived, sir, with a full load of officers from General Headquarters!' he gasped.

Major Mullen sprang to his feet.

'Get back to your stations!' he shouted, making for the door.

Biggles gurgled with glee, as with Mahoney at his side they dashed back to the sheds.

'What a fluke! What an absolute hummer!' he chortled. 'It's a surprise inspection. Won't 301 be pleased when they hear about it!

'They've done us the finest turn they could possibly do for us—if they'd spent a year trying to work it out. The laugh will be on our side, after all.'

An hour later the officers and mechanics of Squadron No. 266 were paraded in front of the sheds, and General Sir Martin Ashby, of the General Headquarters Staff, addressed them.

'It gives me great pleasure,' he began in his stentorian voice, 'to see a squadron in the field that can carry itself with such spotless efficiency. I have visited many units in the course of my duties, but never has it been my lot to find one in which such praiseworthy zeal is so obviously displayed by all ranks.

'Your equipment is a credit to yourselves, your commanding officer, and the Service as a whole. I shall make it my business to see that the magnificent example you have set is made known to every other squadron in France. So gratified am I to find that a unit in this command can maintain itself as I have always claimed that a squadron can be maintained, in spite of active service conditions, that I shall cause these observations to be published tonight in R.F.C. orders, so that all other units on the Western Front* may be aware of the pattern you have set. Thank you!'

Major Mullen's face wore a broad smile as he returned from seeing the officers on their way.

'What a slice of luck!' he laughed. 'The squadron's reputation is now higher than it has ever been before, and the general has just told me that all requests from us will in future receive his personal consideration. Applications for leave will receive priority.

'Yes, the laugh is certainly with us. What is more, I took the opportunity of mentioning Lacey's little episode, and the general has promised to put the matter right with Wing, which means that no further action will be taken in the matter, except that Captain Bitmore is likely to get a rap over the knuckles. In fact, everything seems to have panned out extremely well!'

---

* The front line trenches stretching from the North Sea to the Swiss frontier where the opposing armies faced one another.